1

THE GIRL ON THE MOOR

A GOTHIC TALE

Phil Page

Printed in the United Kingdom

First Printing, 2020

ISBN 978-1-78723-365-2

Published by Completely Novel.com

www.philpage.org.uk

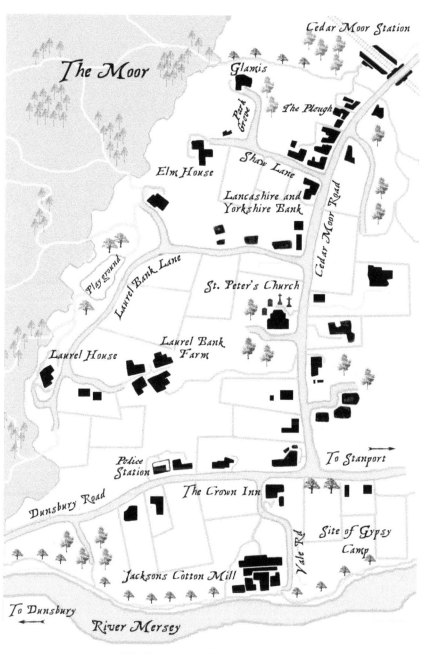

Cedar Moor 1900

Shadows

Even as a young child I was never fearful of shadows. I marvelled at their fitful shapes cast onto the living room walls by the flames that licked and twisted in the metal grate. In the wild summer storms, they were flickering fragments darting across my bedroom window and racing frantically between the trees and across the lawn. In the calm of night, they crept almost imperceptibly around my bedroom as the moon continued its constant journey across the clear, night sky.

I often dreamed of what would happen if I caught one. Would it writhe and twist in my grip, its grotesque form struggling to escape from my clutches? Or would it encompass me and draw me into its eerie, silent world where I would become a servant of the night until the fading darkness released me into an empty dawn?

In my childish imagination I believed they were alive, sinister reflections cast from creatures lurking beyond my vision. I would try to trace them to their source, innocently believing that I would enter a hidden hollow in the garden where they would lie waiting to draw me into their world of stealth, secrecy, and invulnerability.

Gleefully, I would hide inside them, waiting for my sister to enter my room or turn a corner in the garden. Then I would leap from their protection, emerging like some ravenous creature seeking its prey, and she would run screaming to our mother who would tell her to be brave and not to be disturbed by such mischief.

I believed the ancient tale that, away from the light, deep within a shadow's veil, humans were immune to attack from supernatural entities either in this world or the next.

Although their shape and form would change, they were always there, waiting, watching, protectors of my world.

I was at one with shadows. They were my companions and friends. They held no sinister fears for me; until she came.

Chapter 1
Cedar Moor

Today was not a day for distant travelling. There would be no express train sweeping me from the city, thundering across the countryside and racing through small, provincial stations. There would be no fleeting glimpses of place names, gated level crossings or children waving excitedly from sunlit embankments. The dark body of the engines, the smell of hot oil, and a breath of warm ash in the air kindled my childhood memories. Those were happy and peaceful days with my family but today I stood alone, shivering on the concourse of Manchester's London Road Station. For some hours the rain had been relentless, and I was glad of the shelter from one of those wet, northern days where the sky descends to coat familiar streets and landmarks in a dreary haze.

I stood for a moment and watched the blur of activity swirl around me. Passengers moved swiftly in a swarm of purposeful chaos, scurrying to board lines of carriages which stretched away towards distant engines fired with restless impatience as they waited to depart. Above them, a threatening sky grumbled and sheets of rain swept across the arched canopy of steel and glass. From a nearby platform a train pulled away, only to be swallowed by the creeping mists as it left the sanctuary of the station.

The attendant clipped my ticket and I made my way to Platform 10 where an ageing saddle tank engine waited with its three coaches ready to undertake the short journey to Stanport. My destination was the penultimate stop, Cedar Moor, a small, thriving village just two miles to the north of the town. I settled into a second-class compartment and presently the first abrupt jolt of the carriage signalled the start of my journey and a welcome relief from the bustle and noise of the adjacent platform.

The train moved from the cover of the station's canopy, allowing slivers of grey light to steal into the small, six-seat compartment. My only travelling companion was a smartly dressed man of around fifty years, and we nodded politely to each other in acknowledgement that our journey had commenced.

'Terrible weather,' the stranger grumbled before rumbles of thunder, and the battering of rain on the windows, curtailed any further chance of conversation.

Snaking south from the city, the railway had altered the character of Cedar Moor significantly. For some years it had been a modest, rural village set on the banks of the Mersey, its inhabitants scraping a paltry existence through farming the poor land which straddled a ridge overlooking the Cheshire Plain. It was a place of hovels, barns and tithe cottages. It was home to farmhands and their families and hosted a transient population of seasonal workers. It was a place of old stories, prejudices and a suspicion of anything that might upset the precarious nature of existence. The shadow of being banished from a meagre security into the workhouse, or onto the streets as a wandering beggar, hanging on the whim of a local farmer or landlord.

Now it was different. Now there were parks, fashionable shops and a smattering of industrial enterprises on the banks of the river. A sizeable housing stock had grown outwards from the station. It was home to bankers, businessmen and entrepreneurs who chose to live in this fresh new environment a few minutes ride from the commercial heart of a great city.

I wiped away some of the condensation which was forming on the carriage window but, as the train rattled south, there was little to suggest that the storm swirling across the industrial outskirts of the city would abate and afford me a clearer view of The Pennines which were barely visible behind the mills, factories and grim rows of terraces. With each gust of wind, small patches of green became momentarily visible before a driving curtain of rain turned the landscape to a weathered grey.

Nonetheless, the wretched conditions could do nothing to dampen my spirits. In my briefcase, I had a letter from the Lancashire and Yorkshire Bank confirming my appointment as assistant manager at their local branch in Cedar Moor and I had secured excellent lodgings nearby. Clara Jackson, whom I hoped to marry, lived in Cedar Moor with her parents, and twin sister Grace, in Elm House, a fine Victorian villa built by her father a decade ago. The house was only a short walk from the station and it was the only part of the village with which I was acquainted. On my visits I had been allowed only to stroll across to the Moor with Clara and share an afternoon tea with the family before leaving to make the tiresome journey back to my family home in Bolton.

I opened my briefcase and took out a photograph, looking contentedly at the young, fresh-faced woman, with flowing brown hair, who had changed the direction of my life so dramatically. Clara had grown up in the village and had amused me with the stories of the old days, picked up from those who had remained and could recount the timeworn tales.

A body of some despairing soul pulled from the river, a victim robbed in some dark lane at night. These were the consequences of inescapable poverty. But there were well-held beliefs less easily attributed to the despondency and depression of the daily struggle to survive. Linger too long on the Moor after the dimming of the day, they said, and you will be drawn into the soul of the land. The dark woodland will close in on your spirit with a suffocating and unpredictable intent. I smiled and returned the photograph to my briefcase. The stories left me in a state of amusement. I liked to consider myself a man of the new century and that the embellished tales of a different generation bore no relevance to me. Still, I was keen to get to know the area and I was taken with its curious air of mystery.

Clara and I had met just over a year ago at a clients' dinner held by the bank in the grandeur of the Midland Hotel in the heart of the city. It was one of those chance encounters which could have been undone by any number of the twists and turns of fortune which determine the destiny of your life.

At first, we exchanged embarrassed glances, but as the evening developed, we chatted and took to dancing. When I discovered that her father was Joseph Jackson I immediately felt that I was possibly aspiring above my station. I knew he was the owner of a cotton mill on the banks of the River Mersey and that he also ran a large and profitable property company. Substantial amounts of his capital contributed to the bank's standing in local financial circles and I was wary of how he would feel about someone from the lower ranks of commerce making advances to his daughter. However, by the end of the evening, I had been introduced and warmly invited for a Sunday tea. On that occasion I found Joseph to be welcoming and hospitable but, as my acquaintance with him developed, I discovered that he was a man of many faces and that the one he presented to you was not always the most genuine.

I had to admit, he grew to be one of my least favoured of people. I considered myself to be a conscientious worker, someone who could consider the needs of both sides in a financial transaction but Joseph was a man who demanded success. He knew nothing less. He was a man of short stature, but his personality dominated every occasion. At home, he revelled in being the centre of attention, boasting about his achievements and his success in affording his family comfort and wealth. In business he was aggressive, ruthless, and not content unless a deal was secured at the expense of a lesser rival. He delved only into your world to seek reassurance that you were worthy of his acquaintance and that you shared his views on business, politics and religion.

Nonetheless, I hoped that now my career was on an upward trajectory, the moment might be close where he might finally agree to us becoming engaged. On my last visit I had found the courage to ask him for Clara's hand in marriage. He had not dismissed my request but had insisted that he needed time to reflect on what would be best for his daughter. I took this to mean that he would be considering my financial position and future prospects as well as the social standing of my family. Despite his indecision, I was confident that I would meet his expectations. My father was a respected civil engineer who had worked on several constructions for the Lancashire and Yorkshire Railway and my mother came from a prosperous Lancastrian family. I had career aspirations and, if my plans were successful, in a couple of years' time, I would have a reasonable measure of financial independence, enough perhaps to secure a mortgage on one of the solid, respectable houses which were a feature of Cedar Moor. More than anything, I wanted to create a new life for us both, and free Clara from the overbearing influence of her father.

Despite the ominous nature of the weather, these thoughts of future happiness filled me with inner warmth. Clara and I would start from modest beginnings and build our lives together through our determination and independence. Neither of us desired the privileges gifted to his two eldest daughters. Rosie and Hattie had been provided for; eased into lives of financial security by Joseph's overseeing eye. They were already married to men of substantial means. Rosie's husband, Richard Dagworth, dealt in stocks and shares and owned a sizeable property in the wealthy village of Bramhall. Hattie lived in similar comfort on the edge of Cedar Moor, for her husband, Howard Longman, was the managing director of a successful engineering company.

As we approached the station, the rain and wind rattled the carriage window, and I pulled the collar of my overcoat tight in preparation for the half-mile walk to my lodgings. The gusts strengthened, whipping up leaves and other loose material from the trackside, creating momentary whirlwinds of debris which were sucked into the slipstream of the train and cast across my view. Then, with a heave and a series of metallic jolts, the train screeched to a halt on the wet rails and the red and white station sign heralded my arrival at Cedar Moor.

I bade my travelling companion good day, and moments later I was alone on the platform, the engine hissing and spitting as if trying to disgorge more passengers from the comfort of its carriages onto the wet expanse of the platform which offered only a flat, shimmering reflection of the grey emptiness above.

For a few seconds the warmth from the engine sheltered me from the bitterness of the day, but the force of the storm was such that it was quickly banished leaving me open to the full force of the rain which cascaded from the heavens. My cosy musings of future plans were replaced with a sense of empty foreboding and almost before I could acquaint myself with the surroundings, I felt something within me change. I had a sinking sense of loss as if I had left a priceless fraction of my life on the train. The comfort of the yellow-lit compartments seemed to beckon me back but the train slipped away into the gathering darkness, disappearing amongst clouds of steam, and my mind felt drained almost to the point of desolation. Something seemed to have invaded my very being and in an instance enticed the feelings of happiness from my soul. The station felt forsaken as if I had arrived at the very end of existence itself, but I had an overpowering feeling that I was not alone

As I stood thumbing my pockets for the ticket that would allow me to exit the platform and climb the steep, canopied stairwell up to the road, my gaze was drawn to the brickwork rising from the edge of the steps. A weak lamp illuminated the exit but on the far wall was a shadow of exaggerated definition given the poor quality of the light. I wiped the rain from my eyes and looked closer. As I gazed across, it seemed to move, creating an outline across the stairs and wall. It was first one shape and then another, an amorphous puzzle which drew my attention from the sheets of mist and rain which drove unforgivingly into my face.

Then, for a brief moment, it fixed on the wall. I perceived it to be cloaked with wisps of black hair flowing around a hood. My first impression was that of a child, a girl, perhaps of some eight or nine years, but I was too far removed from the exit to make a reliable judgement. I quickly reasoned that my eyes were searching for something which could not exist and that personifying the abstract shapes of shadows was one of my childhood fancies. For a moment the clouds parted, causing a dramatic shift in the direction of the light and, as I peered again, the dark outline had been absorbed into the flat shadow of the wall. The apprehension I had felt when alighting from the carriage began to diminish and keen to escape the rain, which was now becoming incessant, I took a few paces towards the exit. However, suddenly the sense of unease rose again.

As the clouds gathered and the darkness grew once more, the shape reappeared, turned, skipped effortlessly up into the hollow of the stairwell and quickly disappeared from view. Feeling momentarily light-headed, I grasped the side of a nearby bench, steadying myself in an attempt to regain my composure. The last wisps of steam from the engine cleared, and a hand clutched at my arm.

'Are you all right, sir?'

It was the reassuring voice of the stationmaster. He offered me a handkerchief, and I mopped the sweat and the rain from my face as he guided me to shelter beneath the canopy of the waiting room.

'This may seem strange, but did you see anyone on the stairwell?'

'See who, sir?'

'Possibly a girl. I thought I saw the shape of a young girl in the darkness behind the gate.'

He looked puzzled and carefully gazed along the length of the platform and towards the steps which led up and away from the station.

'There is no one, sir. Neither has there been anyone here for a good half hour. No one can get onto this platform without my permission. Have you far to go? Shall I call a cab?'

'No. No thank you.'

I stuffed my ticket into his hand made for the exit.

Then, as I hastened up the stairs I became aware of a sound echoing in the chamber. It was impossible to pinpoint its source but I was sure it was a child's laughter. Helpless giggling as might be made in the turmoil of play when a child realises it can no longer evade the chase of someone in breathless pursuit. Then there was the quick pattering of footsteps above me, followed by silence.

I ran, climbing the steps at such speed that by the time I reached street level my heart was pounding and I was gasping uncomfortably for breath.

The road was straight in both directions. Blurred figures hastened about their business, half-hidden by the driving rain. But there was no child. If one existed, it had now disappeared into the pale light of the bleakest of days.

Chapter 2
Edith Murdstone

After chiding myself for allowing my fatuous imagination to divert my attention from the affairs of the real world, I hailed a Hansom cab and directed the driver to the address written in my notebook. I gathered my thoughts, suggesting to myself that, after the excitement and anticipation of the journey, the sudden transition from the warmth of the carriage into the constricting coldness of the day, had drained my strength creating unwelcome feelings of detachment and unease. I had possibly seen a young girl but if so, she was most likely a street urchin who had crept unnoticed past the stationmaster in the hope of securing any small token of generosity from the alighting passengers. The sounds within the stairwell had been a fusion of echoes gathering from the station platform and the road above.

We trotted at a steady pace along Cedar Moor Road, past a row of shops whose frontages were sheltered by an ornate glass and iron arcade which ran the length of the parade. Given that it was Sunday no trade was in progress but I noted that there were sufficient businesses to provide the essential services which would alleviate the need for local residents to undertake regular journeys into Manchester or Stanport.

There was a chemist, butcher, greengrocer, ironmonger and two or three shops selling fancy goods. The shops were well-kept, their windows and shutters enriched with fresh paint. At the end of the row was a large milliner's selling hats, its windows full of bonnets, lace caps, trilbies, cloth caps and boaters. There were several elegant hats of the type favoured by well-to-do ladies, adorned with ribbons, flowers, feathers and jewels. I wondered how they secured the trade in such a small village. I would no doubt have time to find out for next door stood the Lancashire and Yorkshire Bank.

As we turned sharply past the shops, we followed a course parallel with the Moor; the wild expanse of green space from which the village derived its name. I felt suddenly distanced from the comfort of the village, taken by its size and the expanse of darkness which swallowed what traces of daylight remained. I was aware that it spread south until it bordered local farmland before dropping away, following the River Mersey, and reaching the outskirts of Dunsbury Village some two miles to the west. The Moor was full of trees, hidden pathways and more formal recreational areas. Clara said it featured in many of the old tales. It was said that when the mist descended, and the silence settled in its hollows, spirits were released from the ground looking to inhabit the bodies of those lost in the dim light, taking their souls and once more entering the world of the living. Some lived with the belief that the Moor was alive, a slumbering presence which felt the pulse of all who cared to hurry across its surface. In the quiet times, they said, you could hear it breathe and sense its restless awareness of humans and creatures as they moved across its pathways and through its undergrowth and dense thickets.

I thought of the first time I had encountered it. I had walked a short distance into its denser parts with Clara before she had hesitated to say she would go no further. She said it had swallowed old pathways unused by those wary of following certain ways. They lay hidden in the vegetation. People had forgotten where they led. Some said no one knew, for the unfortunate travellers never returned. The Moor knew of the lure of the path; how the eye and mind are enticed by the prospect of adventure and discovery. She was convinced the stories were too real to be discounted as the unsubstantial witterings of old wives. Perhaps it had been inconsiderate of me to dismiss the folklore of the place.

By the time I arrived at my lodgings my strength was beginning to return. I collected my bag, tipped the driver, and made my way up the gravelled drive of Laurel House, admiring its handsome, red-brick facade and pleasant views across the Moor with its parkland and bowling greens.

'Get inside quickly, Mr Blackwood. You must be cold and weary after travelling in such dreadful weather.'

'Thank you, Mrs Murdstone. You are too kind. I'm looking forward to lodging with you and your family.'

'Oh, there is just me here, now,' she smiled, 'I was happily wedded once but sadly my husband is now gone.' The smile faded and she turned away to close the front door.

She was a short, plump woman in her mid-50s, and did not conform to my expectations of a typical landlady. She was well-dressed and wore the healthy look of a person unburdened by the toils of cooking, washing and cleaning. Her face was soft and displayed hardly any of the signs of ageing a woman might carry into her later years.

The house was bright and welcoming. It felt clean and well-aired and there was the pleasant aroma of fresh flowers. It had been recently decorated and through the doors, which led to the reception rooms, I could see heavy curtains and wallpaper with a floral design. In each room there were thick rugs, tasteful ornaments, paintings and plants. I could feel the warmth of an open coal fire penetrating into the hall.

She helped me out of my damp coat and ushered me into her parlour with the promise that in a few minutes I would be revived with a pot of her finest tea, Imperial Blend, purchased locally at Burgon's Tea Emporium, and as many of her home-baked scones as I would care to consume.

As she departed for the kitchen, I took in the surroundings and my curiosity grew. This was not a home run by a widow of limited wealth whose rent from a lodger would provide only a meagre income with no means to replace ageing furniture and ragged decoration. I supposed that perhaps she had been left a legacy by her husband or inherited money in later life. Conceivably, she continued to take in lodgers for company and to engage in occasional episodes of polite conversation rather than living with the echoes of empty rooms. However, I was glad to be staying in such comfort and it was not my business to speculate on the lives of other people.

We sat and chatted. I told her details of my employment and ambitions, and she was pleased with my references, preferring 'professional types' to passing travellers. I told her nothing of my personal circumstances, not wishing for fragments of gossip to be shared amongst the community for, in my experience, landladies, with their network of friends and tradespeople were prone to embellishing even the most innocent of tales.

Presently, Mrs Murdstone took me to my room. I was glad to see my baggage had arrived safely and was neatly placed next to the wardrobe. I was given an hour to settle in before my presence was required in the parlour to arrange for payment of my rent. Like the rest of the house, the room was furnished seemingly without any concern for expense. The bed was made of the finest oak, and the mattress was filled with duck down and exceedingly comfortable. There was a small, marbled washbasin and a study desk with a comfortable leather chair. The three oil paintings on the walls were all original works by a prominent local artist but my eye was drawn to the desk on which sat a small, framed pencil drawing of the Moor. The outlook was from the front gate of Laurel House and was drawn with an artist's eye, recreating the perspective of the landscape in fine detail. I picked it up and examined it closely. At the end of a path leading away into the Moor were two figures. They seemed to be young children and the difference in their size indicated that one was older. They were pictured hand in hand, one leading the other away from the artist's viewpoint. The picture had a melancholy atmosphere which reached from the frame into the mind of the observer. It was simply signed, 'Edith'. My landlady was a woman of some artistic talent.

After unpacking my things, I wandered outside. The rain had stopped, and a pale light was easing through gaps in the clouds. I walked around the garden admiring the fine array of plants and the immaculately cut lawn and borders. The autumn air was fresh and reviving, and I had an overwhelming feeling that my stay here would be a happy one.

I gazed across the Moor. The stroll to see Clara after a day's work would be a pleasant reward. Areas of it had been well-developed by the Parish Council and, in addition to two bowling greens, there was a bandstand, a playground, an aviary, tree-lined pathways and expanses of lawn where families could picnic and allow their children to run freely. However, this afternoon it was quiet and, apart from two sombrely dressed women walking their dogs, no one else was to be seen. I checked my watch. At five o'clock, on the afternoon of a weekend, I would have expected more activity but, there again, the weather had been miserable and perhaps it was too late in the day for people to be drawn from the comfort of their homes and preparations for a Sunday tea.

I looked back towards the path, but the two women had gone. Suddenly, my gaze was drawn towards the trees. I thought I caught a fleeting movement as if something had darted quickly across the periphery of my vision. The wind caught the leaves casting rippled movements of light across the outline of the avenues, and I thought it carried a sound, a murmured cry which almost reached my ears before dropping away, lost in the silence of its lonely hollows. I squinted hard, looking into the failing light of the afternoon. There was nothing. The rain started to fall once more. I turned and walked back into the house.

Mrs Murdstone sat at her bureau surrounded by a cluster of papers and stationery. I signed my lodging agreement and paid her a month's rent in advance. She placed the money carefully in an envelope and left to lock it in her filing cabinet which she informed me was in the cellar. I took a small notebook from my pocket intent on entering the date and amount I had paid, but I could find no trace of a pen in any of my pockets. Noticing the pot of pens and pencils on the bureau, I eased myself into her chair and took an expensive-looking fountain pen from the pot. I was about to update my notebook when an old, brown envelope in the corner of the desk caught my eye. It was addressed to Edith Murdstone, before her marriage, and not at the house in which I sat. I picked it up and read the details:

Miss Edith Wood
Personal Assistant to Joseph Jackson
Shaw House
Park Grove
Cedar Moor

The date on the stamp was from the summer of 1880, some twenty years previous. I was indeed curious. However, I reasoned that the fact that I had found myself residing with a former employee of Joseph Jackson nothing more than a passing coincidence.

After a hearty meal of beef, vegetables, potatoes and gravy, I settled in the parlour for about an hour, checking my documentation from the bank in preparation for the first day of my new employment. At around ten o'clock I retired to my room. As I closed the curtains, I noticed fragments of light from the gas lamp dancing between the shadows across the entrance to the fields. I opened the sash window slightly and listened. The Moor was silent. The unsettled conditions of the day had passed, and an innocent moon was peering through the damp air which was settling on the roofs and pavements. I slowly drew the curtains and retired to the comfort of my bed.

.

.

Chapter 3
Engagement

The Lancashire and Yorkshire Bank was set in the heart of Cedar Moor village and provided the means for local publicans, grocers, ironmongers, haberdashers, chemists and other more cosmopolitan businesses to manage their financial affairs, overseen by Mr Charles Tomkins, the branch manager.

Having previously met Mr Tomkins at my appointment, I was well aware of his obsession with order and efficiency. He was an ex-army man who had moved into banking after a stray bullet in the first Boer conflict had splintered his left kneecap. His mobility was now heavily reliant on a wooden walking stick which he seemed to enjoy pointing at employees to emphasise his views about responsibilities, smart dress and customer relations.

He was short and stout and gave the impression that he had just been on a short run or indulged in some other form of brisk exercise which had overexerted him. His forehead bore a film of sweat which he tried to clear by regular wipes with the large handkerchief located in his rear trouser pocket. His cheeks seemed to be permanently bloated and red, and when he spoke there was a constant wheeze as he fought to squeeze out his words between steady gasps of air.

Even though the weather was chill, he had removed his jacket to reveal a finely-tailored waistcoat with a gold chain and watch fob which he held in the flat of his hand.

'Bang on time, Mr Blackwood. Splendid! Presence and punctuality. Clients should never be left waiting. Sit down, my good man.' He directed me to the plush, leather chair which faced across his desk. 'Welcome to the Lancashire and Yorkshire.' He tapped his walking stick sharply on the wooden floor. 'Expectations! That's what we have to live up to here. There's new wealth in this community. Wealth and influence.' He smiled, tapping his stick again as if to emphasise his point.

'We are the small bank with big responsibilities. Savings, investments, loans, inheritance. Our customers are our friends. Confidence and confidentiality. We give the utmost professional advice on all things financial. It's what the customers expect. Is that clear?'

'Yes, sir.'

'And something of paramount importance.' He softened his tone and leaned towards me, conversing in almost a whisper, as if fearful that the ears of an unwelcome listener might be pressed against the door of his office. 'During certain meetings where we give financial, and often necessary personal advice, some of our clients may well divulge things to you which, how can I put it, are not necessarily of a banking nature. Then we must be listeners, counsellors, confidantes. Whatever is disclosed must never be discussed with anyone in this branch, or outside within your personal circle of family and friends. Do you understand?'

I was not entirely sure what he meant, but I gave him my word which he seemed happy to accept without any further interjections. Thirty minutes later my induction into the world of provincial banking was complete. I had a file of customers, for whose financial affairs I would be responsible, a list of meetings for the coming week and my administrative duties for each day. My attendance in the office would cease at midday on Fridays after which I would accompany Mr Tomkins to the Plough Hotel for drinks and what he described as, 'a working lunch with valued clients.' He also left me in no doubt about my future career prospects, advising me that his knee was deteriorating rapidly and that he had recently been in conversation with Head Office about the possibility of retirement. I had been identified as his potential replacement and would receive the benefit of his personal guidance and training which should enable me to step into his shoes in little more than a year.

During my lunch break, my thoughts turned to Joseph and whether he might have made his decision regarding my request to marry his daughter. I was aware that my anxieties were not shared by Clara who displayed a calm confidence that her father was merely deliberating in order to show his control over all family matters.

'As a child, I was never given anything at first asking,' she would smile. 'It will be the same with you, Adam.'

Yet, I worried about how Joseph saw me in comparison to Richard and Howard. They had accrued real wealth through their successful business ventures. Although their after-dinner conversations about stocks, shares and investments allowed me to contribute to the debate, their practical knowledge of the business community fed my feelings of inferiority. I envied their bullishness. They were confident, outgoing and talked to Joseph as equals, playing to his ego by often seeking his advice about buying and selling property.

They were alike in almost every facet of their characters. In their private lives they were purposeful, addressing problems quickly, seeking out speedy resolutions to any issue or decision which might affect the happiness of their existence. Richard, in particular, displayed an overwhelming optimism that everything in life was within his control.

I wondered though, about Rosie and Hattie. Although they were sisters they seemed completely devoid of any common familial traits. Rosie was the elder of the pair by two years but in all aspects of her character seemed younger. She was rounded, healthy, and had a passion for her two children,

Thomas and Victoria. She conversed knowledgeably on many of the social and political issues of the day and was a close companion to her mother. She would go out of her way to engage me in topical conversations, and her smile radiated warmth and happiness. Hattie though was a puzzlement. Here was a woman with a foothold in the higher reaches of middle-class society. She had seemingly everything a young woman could want; a successful husband, a grand house and financial security. Yet she often seemed withdrawn and aloof as if her mind was constantly fixed on thoughts far from the comfort of her daily existence. Her brow was furrowed, and it seemed that the criss-cross of lines had been forged by unrelenting periods of worry and anxiety. She shied away from family talk often deflecting the topic of conversation to trivial matters such as the state of the flowerbeds or some gossip she had picked up in her social circle.

Although she was nearing her twenty-eighth birthday and was into her eighth year of marriage to Howard, they had no children. I was fully aware that some couples were destined to remain childless despite their desire to conceive and considered that this might be the overriding reason for her indifferent view of the world. Whatever the reasons, in the company of adults, she was a silent listener. I wondered if she was once like Clara and Grace whose youthful vibrancy embraced those in their company and whose thirst for life and new experiences seemed unquenchable.

On my return to the bank, I was summoned by Mr Tomkins into his office. Seated next to his desk was Joseph Jackson. He rose swiftly and shook me by the hand. There was a mellow look on his face. Something I had not seen on many occasions over the past year.

Without any form of greeting, he addressed me directly.

'Charles tells me that your prospects with the bank are promising.' He glanced across at Mr Tomkins who affirmed his statement with a polite nod and the customary tap of his stick. 'Clara will be pleased, and we will be delighted if you would join us for dinner this evening.'

'Thank you, sir. And I'm pleased to be lodging with Mrs Edith Murdstone, who you will know as Miss Edith Wood. I believe she was once your personal assistant.'

I instantly felt that I had said something inappropriate; that I was in possession of some knowledge of which I had no right to release into a public conversation. I felt like an idiot, but it was impossible to take it back.

Joseph looked momentarily unsettled. He breathed deeply and looked at Mr Tomkins and then back at me. 'She is no longer with me, Adam. She left my employment some twenty years ago.'

Without any further comment, he shook Mr Tomkins' hand and left.

Almost immediately, Mr Tomkins became noticeably agitated. He padded around the room, gasping and wheezing, tapping his stick rapidly and gazing out of the window at Joseph who was moving hurriedly down the drive.

'How on earth did you know that?' There was a slight aggressiveness in his voice which was at odds with his pleasant demeanour of the previous hours.

'Just a letter on her bureau. I saw the writing by chance. It was addressed to her with her title as Mr Jackson's personal assistant.'

Mr Tomkins turned, raised his stick and pointed it towards my chest. It was almost touching my jacket, and for a moment I feared he was about to force me back across the room.

'Confidentiality! There are things which can be said and things that should remain buried. You have a lesson to learn, Adam, if you are to be accepted into our community.'

He took his handkerchief from his back pocket and drew it slowly across his brow. His gaze left mine and he lowered himself into his leather chair. He took a pen from his drawer and opened a ledger. He made a short entry on one of the pages and looked back up at me. 'No matter, Adam. Get back to your desk.'

* * * * * *

After work, I washed, shaved and dressed in my best suit in readiness for my evening meal with Clara and her family. The walk across the Moor was pleasant, and I was in good spirits following Joseph's surprisingly positive response to my career prospects. However, I was concerned about the possible impact of my revelation about Edith Murdstone and whether Mr Tomkins' reaction indicated that I had indiscreetly broken his rule about professional confidentiality. Perhaps she had left his employment under a cloud or more likely it was his usual cursory response to anything which no longer concerned him. Whatever the reason it was no concern of mine and I was not the type of person who took pleasure from unravelling the details of people's private business.

I left the Moor and made my way up the gravel drive of Elm House. Joseph had commissioned the building himself, and it was as fine an example of a Victorian villa as one could imagine. It was built attractively in Accrington red brick with a central gabled roof which contained portions of black and white Tudor cladding. It sat on the northern edge of the Moor in a substantial plot of land and was visible from some distance across the farmland and golf course which stretched north towards the outline of the city. I ventured up the drive past the two sets of mullioned windows which were a feature of the hallway and rang the bell. I was welcomed at the front door by Hannah, their maid, and escorted into the morning room where Howard, Richard and Joseph were sharing an aperitif of brandy and smoking extraordinarily large cigars.

'Adam! Welcome! Welcome!' Joseph clutched my hand, shaking it intensely and motioning to Hannah to pour me a brandy. There seemed to be no reaction to our meeting a few hours ago. If anything, his demeanour was more affable, and he appeared genuinely happy to greet me. A crystal glass was swiftly placed into my hand, and for a moment, the conversations subsided before Joseph spoke.

'A toast!' He raised his glass, motioning to Richard and Howard to do the same. 'To our family,' he smiled, 'and everything that wealth and happiness can bring to our lives.'

We smiled and drank from our glasses. Joseph motioned to Hannah, and they were filled again.

'And now, to Adam,' he continued, nodding towards Richard and Howard. 'As you will all know, I am no stickler for formalities. Matters of business should be dealt with swiftly. Clara has been the picture of happiness from the moment she first met Adam. I can think of no better person with whom she might spend the rest of her life.' He raised his glass majestically. 'So, I offer up a toast. To your future brother-in-law and my future son-in-law.'

The glasses were raised, emptied, and suddenly my hand was being shaken, and stout words of congratulation were echoing around the room. From behind the curtain, at the rear of the room, came Clara, Rosie, Hattie, Grace and Mary, their mother, and I was overwhelmed by tearful hugs and kisses and Clara's hand held mine as if she would never let go.

I had little recollection of the flow of the conversation around the dinner table save that Clara had already considered a date for the wedding. It would take place at St Peter's Church on May 16th, 1901 with Grace as chief bridesmaid and Rosie and Hattie in support. After our marriage, we would move into the spare rooms at Elm House until such time as we were able to afford our own home. The atmosphere was heady and the infusion of sudden happiness and the effect of several glasses of wine, followed by port and more brandy, had left me in a state of befuddlement. On one hand, I was delighted at the prospect of marrying Clara but on the other, I felt a certain resentment at the nature of Joseph's announcement. He had orchestrated it all to steal the moment and make himself the centre of attention. I felt as if I was a piece of a jigsaw puzzle which he was intent on completing. Only Grace was left now and no doubt he was already searching for the last piece to make his picture of family happiness complete.

The room was a babble of noise and celebration. I needed air and hurriedly made an excuse to leave the table. Nobody showed any concerns, and the conversations continued unabated. I half stumbled into the hall and down the corridor to the front door. The night air filled my lungs providing an antidote to the clouded state of my mind. I managed to clear my head and relaxed, with the sudden realisation that all my hopes and dreams were coming to fruition and that this evening was the first step in mine and Clara's life together.

Across the road, the Moor was dark and silent as the stillness of the autumn evening settled along its deserted pathways. Nothing stirred, and after the clamour and celebration of the previous hour, it seemed the perfect space in which to collect my thoughts. I walked slowly through the gate into the blackness.

A low mist was forming on the lawns and across the children's playground, muffling the sound of my shoes as I strolled towards the park keeper's hut. Then came the whispered words travelling through the darkness, barely audible against the creaking of the bare trees. I strained to make sense of them. 'Help me! Help me!' I couldn't be sure. The words seemed to emanate from the shadows, but they were masked by the force of the blood pounding in my ears. I ran towards them trying to gauge from whence exactly they came but as suddenly as they had formed they dissolved and were drawn away into the mist.

I breathed deeply again, imploring myself not to panic, convincing myself that, in the thin night air, the ability of sound to travel considerable distances was an unquestionable fact. They were most probably the sounds of night creatures brought from their hides by the absence of human company in the park. Their cries had been a warning against my presence. I turned, the panic subsiding as I made for the lights of Elm House. As I approached the gates, one last sound made me turn and stare back into the emptiness. It was unmistakably the constant squeak of a metal swing rocking back and forth in the children's playground. It was followed by the faint sound of a child's laughter which faded into the silence of the night.

I hurried back into the dining room, bid Hannah pour me a full measure of brandy, and returned to my place at the table. Clara smiled and took my arm, but her gaze turned instantly to one of concern as she felt the trembling which had already resulted in several drops of brandy shaking from my glass and tumbling onto the tablecloth.

'Be calm, Adam. Father is not such an ogre. Our family may seem a little daunting, but you have nothing to worry about.'

Her smile returned and the evening continued in its whirl of celebration. At midnight I bid everyone farewell and prepared for my short journey across the Moor. Trying to suppress a sense of foreboding, I quickened my pace along the path which was now lit by a hazy moon.

However, my journey passed without incident and back at Laurel House, I reasoned with myself that I had nothing tangible on which to reflect. The sounds could all have been imagined and it was pointless trying to add substance to things which most probably emanated from my anxieties. Nevertheless, that evening I extinguished the lights in my room, parted the curtains, opened the window and waited, listening for the slightest murmur which might drift across the Moor. The minutes passed but there was nothing, except for the recurrent hoot of a night owl sitting silhouetted against a watery moon.

.

Chapter 4
Shadows On The Moor

I had slept deeply and, although there was dragging tiredness in my bones and my mind required liberation from a self-induced lethargy, there was much to consider. On Saturday my parents would travel to Elm House for the first meeting of the two families and I hoped no unresolved tensions would arise, particularly from mothers whose protectiveness towards their children can sometimes overreach the bounds of sensibility. There would be a formal engagement party to organise and consideration of who would be invited and who would not. And then there was the buying of the ring. I had been saving steadily to prepare for the purchase and a quick check of my bank account revealed my finances to be in good shape.

Despite the pressures and demands that our impending marriage would bring, I was in high spirits as I tidied my paperwork, bid Mr Tomkins and the staff good evening, and made my way home. The rain was beginning to swirl in sheets and the light diminishing so I sheltered for a few minutes under the metal and glass arcade of the nearby shops before a temporary abatement of the conditions persuaded me to hurry briskly down one of the side roads and onto the Moor.

Across the bowling greens, I could see the lights of the large houses which bordered the golf course and, as the rain turned to a soft drizzle, I pulled up the collar of my coat and strode purposefully towards Laurel House. As I had been late returning from Elm House the previous evening, I was yet to inform Mrs Murdstone of my good fortune.

The Moor was again silent save for the late afternoon calling of a female blackbird which I could barely see as the rain produced a curtain of mist which turned my view into an indistinct blur. Then the feeling returned. The sudden emptiness, as if all life had been drained from the world and I was alone in an empty space the comforting parameters of existence banished away.

As I struggled to gaze through the damp veil, the wind suddenly parted the thin drizzle, and there was the shape appearing in the mist directly within my field of vision, writhing and shifting between the shadows of the trees but unmistakably the presence from the station platform. It twisted and moved in the light, merging with the shadows and then re-forming with every gust of wind and bending of the trees. In phases the shape became more defined as the light fell upon it and within moments it had stretched into human form, again resembling that of a young girl. In the shadow of the hood, I thought I could make out pale features and shining strands of black, lustrous hair. It did not attempt to move towards me or engage in conversation.

Again the rain clouded my vision, but I swore I could feel eyes fixed upon me, with what purpose I could not imagine. We were some twenty yards apart, and my instinct was to turn and flee, but before I could gather myself to act a piercing growling and then barking caused me to turn sharply. A black hound, its coat matted with rain and its jaws dripping with saliva, bounded towards me as if intent on inflicting me some harm. However, in moments, it was past me, and I turned again. The shape had gone; the dog scratching and howling at the spot on which it had materialised. A well-dressed young man, hurried towards me, an empty lead trailing from his hand.

'My apologies, sir. She slipped the leash. She's harmless really. I hope she caused you no alarm.'

They moved away, the dog loping around the edges of the pathway pursuing the lingering smells of other creatures before it stopped, turned and again ran at some speed towards me, hurtling past and plunging headlong into the undergrowth. For a few moments, it completely disappeared, and all I could hear was scuffling and panting as it scrabbled around between the roots and stems. Then it reappeared. Clutched in its mouth was a ball, but it was no child's plaything. It was of the type used by jugglers in a circus, round and soft with red and gold edging. It sat compressed between the jaws of the animal, and I moved to try to take it, but the dog backed away with a muffled growl and trotted towards its master. I looked into the shadows and for a moment wanted to believe I might dare to reach into the darkness. Instead, I ran, reaching Laurel House in only a few minutes. I hurried to my room and shut the door, grabbed pen and paper from my briefcase, breathed deeply several times, and forced the pen to sketch the image which was fixed in my memory.

I drew swiftly and carefully trying to recreate the detail of its appearance as faithfully as my shaking hands would allow. There was the hair, long and dark, framing the smooth white complexion of a face. I drew the eyes recreating the gaunt stare, but how I could replicate feelings in two-dimensional form. How could the fear she released be recreated on a simple blank page? How could the power which drained my resolve be pictured in a sketch no matter how detailed the corporeal image?

I struggled on to the point where I could not be sure if I was adding details which were, in my desperate urgency to record its identity, imagined rather than accurately reproduced from the fleeting moments of its appearance. However, in a matter of minutes, the drawing was complete.

It was detailed enough to convince myself that I had witnessed the incarnation of a child of some eight or nine years, dressed in black, the paleness of her complexion in stark contrast with the dark garments which cloaked her body. I hurried down to the dining room where I found Mrs Murdstone arranging a single table for my evening meal.

'I need to ask you something.' There was a wavering urgency in my voice which took her attention, and she looked at me with some concern. I passed the sketch to her and guided her to the last vestiges of evening light which crept through the window.

'Do you recognise her?' I could not bring myself to say 'it' and reveal my sense of disquiet to her. 'I think I've seen her in the dimness on the Moor. Do you think she lives in the area? I'm concerned that a girl so young should be out alone and ill-dressed for such bitter weather.'

Mrs Murdstone took her glasses from her pocket and stared hard at the sketch, then placed it firmly on the table.

'Travellers' children. We see them regularly. They camp down by the river. Good supply of water for their horses, washing and other things I don't care to mention. Gypsies regularly come for the horse fairs. Circus people once or twice a year. I've seen lots of children. Parents, if they have any, don't keep an eye on them and next thing you know they're littering the streets, leaping from the shadows, begging, trading, trying to sell you cheap trinkets and baubles. They'll have your money from you before you know it. Either that or they'll leave you with some fearful curse if you don't give them a penny or two.'

'It's not just her appearance, though. When I encountered her, I had these morbid feelings of fear and unease. Feelings I've never encountered before, a kind of draining of my soul as if all my spirit was being stolen from my body.'

40

Mrs Murdstone looked at me understandingly. 'You've been focusing your mind too hard on your new job, my dear. All those high expectations and your hopes for the future. Try to calm yourself and, if you see the girl again, confront her with some harsh words and a threat that you'll have the police on her trail.'

She waited as if expecting a reply but I had nothing to say. Her assessment was logical, believable. The girl could have been hiding in the shadows and fled in fear of the hound. She could have been from a circus family and dropped the ball in haste. There were trees and bushes which would have moved casting shadows into distracting shapes, tricking my mind, and taking her from my gaze in moments.

I sighed and consigned the drawing to the pocket of my coat.

'You are right. I shall take the matter up with the police in the morning and in the meantime I have some good news to share with you. I have only acquainted you with the details of my professional life but let me share some of my personal plans for the coming months.'

Mrs Murdstone smiled as if she was happy with my sudden shift from apprehension to optimism.

'I would love to hear them, Mr Blackwood.'

'Well, I am to be wed next May. My fiancé is a neighbour of yours, Clara Jackson of Elm House. Last night, her father, Joseph, consented to our marriage.'

My news did not have the expected impact on Mrs Murdstone. She took an intake of breath, as if to speak, but instead took hold of the arm of a chair as if she needed some support.

'I really do not know what to say, Mr Blackwood. What a surprise that you will be marrying into such a wealthy and influential family. Have you thought everything through carefully?'

'Oh, yes. Clara and I have known each other for some time. To be married and share our lives together is what we most definitely want.'

Mrs Murdstone steadied herself, grasped my arm, and spoke quietly.

'Then you have my congratulations, Mr Blackwood, and my prayers that all will be well for you both and that you will be able to look back from the future with no regrets.'

Her response seemed strange considering we were only casually acquainted, but given her previous statement of concern for my well-being I took it as a motherly gesture and decided to think no more of it. I returned to my room and took the sketch of the girl from my jacket. I sat at the table adding a few more details to the general form of the child while her appearance was fresh in my mind. Had I been tricked by the inclement conditions? On both occasions, my vision had been blurred by the rain driving directly into my face. However, tomorrow, I would call in at the police station to ascertain if Mrs Murdstone's observations might be confirmed by the local constabulary.

Chapter 5.
Travellers

My night was restless. I gained only small episodes of sleep as my mind searched for an explanation of the events which had banished the excitement of starting my new job and winning the favour of Joseph Jackson. I considered myself a person of stable mind, one who could rationalise the most unlikely of occurrences and seek out plausible explanations where others would be prone to fantasy or fearful superstition. Yet here I was at 5am on a Saturday morning, drained of the comfort a decent night's sleep. My mind consumed by the recurring vision of a disturbing, dark shape creating a conviction that I had encountered a young girl in a black cloak.

I fought to believe that the clear, unequivocal explanation offered by Mrs Murdstone was the end of the affair. For an hour or more I even rehearsed the very words of warning I should bellow at the child should she come into my presence again. But something ate away at Mrs Murdstone's rationality. If it was a child, there had been no direct approach with energy and guile intent on securing my sympathy through some cheap story or sorrowful tale. The thing in the shadows was an empty, dark, shell; emotionless, silent, and almost wraith-like. I had never thought in any depth about my feelings for religion and its views on the after-life, but a sense of worry had settled into my thoughts. Had I become the focus of a troubled soul? Why was it seeking me out, or was it the Moor itself, resurrecting the spirits so prevalent in the rumours and old tales? If so, then others in the village may have shared my experiences and be actively absorbed in searching for explanations, either rational or hypothetical.

As the thin light of dawn broke above the trees on the Moor, my philosophical nature asserted itself, and I decided a more earthly investigation would be appropriate and inevitably ease my worries. After all, who as a youngster has not been regaled with tales of spectres, phantoms and mysterious apparitions most often with the intent of inflicting fear and horror on an innocent mind? Who has not at some time convinced themselves that they are in the presence of such vile spirits, filling themselves with a self-induced fear based completely on the nonsense fed to them as a child?

However, I knew enough to appreciate that even rational people can feel they have at times felt a presence, often when in a fragile or emotional state. But my life was happy. I felt strong, able to cope with the most demanding of situations and yet, on the two occasions I had encountered the shape, it was as if my resolve had been stripped away leaving me disorientated, confused and, in my own mind, afraid.

I had to convince myself to deal in facts rather than taking speculative journeys into the unknown. I reasoned that I was perhaps becoming too deeply absorbed in my own subjective experiences and over-thinking events which could be explained away perfectly reasonably. If I had encountered a child, she must live locally and perhaps had been reported missing by parents consumed with guilt and anxiety. Surely a young girl would not be lost without some record of a police investigation.

A few hours later, I stepped into Cedar Moor Police Station, my sketch folded neatly inside the pocket of my overcoat. I rang the bell on the desk and waited. On the walls were notices giving details of local petty crimes and rewards for information but nothing more. A burly officer, carrying a large mug of tea, came from out of the back room, and I faced him across the counter.

'What can I do for you, sir?'

I offered my explanation that I had twice possibly encountered a girl, too young to be out alone, inappropriately dressed for damp weather, appearing and disappearing without cause or explanation.

The officer took my sketch and examined it dutifully. He removed a well-used pencil from behind his ear, took a ledger from behind the desk and recorded the details of my sightings along with my occupation and address. When he saw that I was employed at the local bank his interest in my observations rose and he became concerned enough to ring the nearby stations at Dunsbury and Stanport to enquire whether there had been any recent reports of a missing child. There was nothing, and his reasoning echoed that of Edith Murdstone, that the area had a transient population of travellers who camped by the river, appearing and disappearing at will, and whose children might dress in any garments available to them regardless of their suitability.

There had indeed been reports and complaints about such a group over the last fortnight, but they had been moved on only the previous evening, just after the time I had last encountered the girl.

'Most likely you've seen the last of her, sir. They'll be the stragglers from the circus family who were down at the end of Vale Road, near the river, last week. They'll be travelling on to Macclesfield or Northwich. I believe there are shows scheduled for the coming week. They'll soon be drawn away.' He paused and chortled, 'People will sleep easier now. Why don't you take a stroll down and, for your own peace of mind, see if they've all left?'

Vale Road twisted and dipped in a steep, cobbled descent from the southern end of Cedar Moor Village, past the entrance to the cotton mill and on to the banks of the River Mersey. At its highest point, it presented elevated views across the Mersey flood plain to the hills of Alderley in the south.

The air was calm, and I could hear the clatter of clogs as the workers hurried about their toils. Beyond the gates of the factory, a thin plume of smoke stretched unbroken into the clear, autumn sky.

Although it was only 10am on a Saturday, the factory had been in production for some hours. Across the field which sloped up to the ridge and the main road, women and children dressed in white smocks were laying out sizeable sheets of bleached cotton to dry in the sun and wind.

Further on, towards the banks of the Mersey, I came across the purpose of my search. The remains of the circus camp were here. The tracks of horse-drawn carts rutted the damp earth, and a fire still smouldered near the path consuming the remnants of wood, cloth and other material deemed unworthy of transportation to their next destination.

In the corner of the field was a solitary caravan. It was a square red box with 'Bailey Brothers Circus' in peeling white lettering across the top. It had a small, square window on one side and two hatches, possibly where people might make enquiries or buy tickets. The spokes of the wheels were brightly painted in red and gold, providing a contrast with the dowdiness of the construction which sat on the chassis above. A set of worn leather reigns and a heavy harness lay next to the steps which led up to a wooden door. An old horse stood shivering in the cold air close by. There seemed to be no one around as I climbed the steps and knocked.

'Can I help you, mister?'

The voice came from behind the vehicle. It was a woman of perhaps forty years although the ruddiness of her skin with its furrowed creases made her look older. She moved slowly as if suffering from some kind of infirmity.

I took the sketch from my pocket and handed it to her.

'I've seen this girl at the station and on the Moor at the top of the hill. I was wondering if you might know her?'

'Who would want to know?'

'Only me. I was worried about her welfare. She was ill-dressed for such wet weather and she seemed in need of help.'

The woman took a pace towards me, and I could see her hands were trembling. She stopped, fixing me with a baleful gaze. She held up the sketch and ripped it to pieces before hurling it into the smouldering embers of the fire.

'Get away! My husband is on his way back from the river. He'll set the dogs on you.'

She plucked a stick from the fire and waved it at me creating spirals of smoke which stung my eyes and dried the back of my throat. The woman looked possessed as if my drawing of the child had ignited some uncontrollable anger. She uttered no further words but spat and coughed aggressively like a cat forced into a corner by some truculent interloper which had strayed into its territory.

Shaken by her actions, I took heed and walked back up Vale Road until I came to a section of raised ground. I scrambled up a few feet from the road and sat in the late morning sun. Back towards the camp, I could see a man attaching the horse roughly to the caravan. He and the woman seemed immersed in a heated conversation. She was waving her arms and pointing in my direction and, for a moment I feared they might pursue me with the purpose of inflicting some harm. However, she disappeared into the caravan, and a few minutes later it was in motion, rumbling and rolling up the cobbled road towards where I sat.

As it approached, I caught a glimpse of the woman peering through the side window. Her gaze focused on nothing, her features were sombre and grey. I stared hard as the cart laboured past and, for a few moments, I sat in parallel with the moving vehicle. The woman was framed by the window, presented as some artistic representation of hopelessness and despair. In her hands, she held a child's peg doll. It had long strands of dark hair and a cap with a pink ribbon. Its dress gleamed white as light momentarily reached through the window and on the front appeared to be embroidered a red rose on a stem of green leaves.

I watched the cart move slowly away up the cobbled rise of Vale Road and then made my way back towards the river remembering the details of its shape and size so that I might make a sketch when I got back to my lodgings. The campfire was still flickering but plumes of smoke billowed from the hot ashes as the flames died. It thickened the air, giving the campsite a dream-like quality. There was a stillness, an absence of life, save for the scattering of woodland creatures hidden in the undergrowth. I knew not what I was looking for but I could feel a presence, the pull of a life force which had no desire to leave this empty place.

I walked into the smoke, immersing myself in its grey shroud and almost immediately my eyes began to sting and water, causing my sight to blur and distort. Suddenly there was shouting and confusion and shapes hurrying across my field of view. There seemed to be people shifting in and out of focus, and I thought I could hear cries from a woman which sounded like, 'Hurry! Hurry!' I fought to regain my sight and as I blinked hard the caravan was there, its paint fresh and new. I turned, and indistinct shapes were moving in the thicker smoke, disappearing from my vision and stumbling towards Vale Road. Then the smoke cleared, and there was silence. I took a handkerchief from my pocket and wiped my eyes which were running and stinging. Blinking was painful, and it was a few moments before I could gaze fully on the empty scene.

It was then that I noticed the footprints in the soil. It had been a dry morning and the area around the campsite was like soft sand which lay across the scrubland. In places, it was churned into well-trodden pathways but to the side, near to where the caravan had stood, it was less disturbed. Two fresh sets of adult footprints led in the direction of Cedar Moor. They revealed the path taken by a man and a woman who were within close proximity of each other. The woman's footprints were light and broken as if she had been moving and turning quickly but those of the man were steady and pressed much deeper into the sand. They were unmistakably the prints of an adult who was carrying a heavy load. I followed their course to where they stopped as the path gave way to the cobbled surface of Vale Road. I hastened several yards towards the rise in a confused belief that I might see two people at some point in the distance, but there was nothing. The road was empty, and only the sharp shouts of factory workers broke the silence. Suddenly the sky darkened, and a tremendous clap of thunder rolled across the ridge. The heavens opened, and a torrent of rain fell swiftly from the clouds. I turned back towards the camp, reaching the softer ground in moments but to my disbelief, the footprints had been washed away.

In a state of some dishevelment, I reached The Crown public house on Dunsbury Road. I hurried into the bar and shook myself as the landlord looked at me pitifully.

'Caught in the storm, sir. What would you like to warm your bones?'

'Brandy! Brandy! A large glass please.'

I sat at a corner table near the crackling log fire, watching through the window as the rain sent rivulets of water running between the cobbles.

I took a notebook from my pocket. It was thankfully still dry, and I spent a few moments sketching the caravan in some detail before stopping to collect my thoughts and think clearly.

There was no new caravan. The smoke had played tricks with my vision. I had been concentrating on its shape and form, and my mind had projected the image in my head onto the film of water which covered my eyes. The shouts had travelled from the factory which was nearby, and the blurred shapes were undoubtedly caused by my eyelids attempting to wash and clear the dust and smoke from my sight. I drank the brandy and ordered another. I continued to warm by the fire, relaxing and coming to a point of reason with the events. The footprints were undoubtedly real. Only minutes before the couple from the caravan would have been loading their last belongings ready to leave. The man would have been struggling with the heavy harness, leading the horse onto solid ground before he coupled the creature to the caravan.

I tore the page from the book, screwed the paper into a tight ball, and tossed it into the fire.

Chapter 6
Thomas

In the days and weeks that followed, I resolved to put matters to the back of my mind and concentrate on the future. The meeting of our two families had been a cordial occasion. Joseph considered my father, George, to embody the spirit of the age. He had a natural interest in the great constructions of the era and the magnificent edifices of steel created by the great Victorian engineers. My mother, Florence, had enthralled Mary with tales of a childhood in Calder Vale and her spirited adventures amongst the undulating fells and moorland of the Forest of Bowland. Our engagement party was a joyous celebration with friends and family, and Clara's engagement ring of two diamonds intertwined with accent stones was admired by all.

I had spent a stressful afternoon in Manchester fretting that I would make the wrong choice and that Clara would be forced to hide her disappointment. However, the assistant at Hancocks in Manchester assured me that such rings were most popular and represented the joining of two hearts, souls and lives.

My career at the bank was developing well, and Mr Tomkins had already given me responsibility for some of the larger accounts on our books. Cedar Moor was growing in prosperity and there was, without doubt, a good degree of wealth centred around what was fast becoming one of the area's most fashionable villages. The preparations for our wedding day were moving swiftly, instilling a constant air of excitement and anticipation within the walls of Elm House. Joseph, himself, seemed animated and more personable than I had ever known him to be and he approved of my choice of best man.

Dr David Walker was one of my newest clients at the bank. We were of similar age and he had just secured his first job at the surgery in Cedar Moor. We got on instantly and were soon meeting socially, enjoying rounds of golf on the local course or drinking in The Plough before retiring to the Reform Club to engage in several highly competitive games of billiards.

I had introduced him to Clara, who in turn, had acquainted him with Grace, and the two were now as much a couple as Clara and myself. Everything in my life seemed to be on an upward trajectory and the events of my early days in Cedar Moor were being consigned to memory. There had been no more sightings of the mysterious child, or any other inexplicable events, and my pragmatic character had allowed me to dismiss her appearances as casual occurrences which my over-imaginative mind had misinterpreted. She was a travellers' child and was most likely in the caravan which trundled past me on Vale Road some three months ago.

Even before we were wed, there was talk of children amongst the family. Joseph and Mary were loving grandparents who regularly entertained and spoiled their two grandchildren. Today was to be no exception. It was the Sunday before Christmas and, after church, Rosie's children joined us to play in the snow which carpeted the grounds of Elm House. We assembled on the terrace and revelled in the excitement of spoiling the crisp blanket of white which lay across the lawn at the rear of the villa. Rosie had given birth to Thomas and Victoria within the space of two years. Victoria was now a bonny child of eight and Thomas, approaching his tenth birthday, was beginning to display that maturity and inquisitive nature which enables a child to hold conversations with adults as an equal.

As the building of a snowman progressed, I focused my attention on Hattie. She was always expensively dressed and by her husband's side at every family occasion, but there seemed to be the absence of a spark of personality and a reluctance to be drawn into the clamour and excitement of the day. She would occasionally smile knowledgeably at some favourable comment or remark but then her interest would fade and her face would revert to its wearisome façade.

She had edged back towards the terrace doors, close enough to give the impression that she was listening to her husband's conversation with Richard, but watching the children anxiously, clenching and twisting her fingers repetitively as if anticipating some calamitous event that might transpire at any moment.

We enjoyed an hour in the garden dodging snowballs and contributing to the construction of a sizable snowman before Thomas returned to the terrace with his hands stuffed into the pockets of his jacket.

'I'm bored!' he yawned over-exaggeratedly. 'Can we go to the park on the Moor?'

Joseph laughed and patted Thomas on the shoulder.

'Growing out of all this, young man? Why don't you take him across to the playground, Adam? It will allow you to get to know each other better.'

'I don't think so, father,' interrupted Rosie. 'It's getting rather late in the afternoon, and we shall have to get home shortly. The children will be growing tired.'

'Nonsense!' roared Joseph. 'Howard, Richard and I have business matters to discuss and I am ready for a good brandy to warm my bones. You have an hour or so yet, Adam. What do you think?'

As I was obviously excluded from the business matters, and had no desire to linger in the company of five women, I motioned to Thomas and in a few moments, we were striding through the iron gates chattering and laughing as if we had known each other for some time.

'May I call you Uncle Adam, sir, even though you are not yet married to Clara?'

I smiled. 'You may indeed but only if I can call you, Mr Thomas.'

We had struck a friendship, and I mused on my good fortune in becoming a member of a large and spirited family.

Thomas grabbed my hand and dragged me towards the playground. Being a Sunday afternoon, it was busy with several mothers watching their children play on the see-saw and the roundabout. Thomas headed for the swings, leaping excitedly into a vacant seat next to some boys.

The air seemed unusually heavy for winter, and there was a sense of the day closing in. The nooks and hollows of the park were losing their definition as the light began to drop, turning the view across the Moor into a series of dark, undefined shapes. The gathering chill gave the promise of a cold night to come, and the first distant stars were beginning to present themselves in the ice-blue sky. I settled on a nearby bench intent on letting Thomas enjoy himself, free from the ever-watching eye of adults. The repetitive creak of the chains sent me into a reverie, my eyes closed, and time seemed to drift slowly away.

I dozed for what could have been several minutes or even longer, the metronomic creaking of the chains a comforting lull which presented a picture of a child engaged in the act of pure enjoyment, swinging free in the cool, winter breeze.

It was time to go. I opened my eyes to gaze on a deserted playground, the swing creaking and swaying, the seat empty and a torrent of panic coursing through my body. I jumped and looked around. The darkness was gathering and the temperature dropping at a pace.

'Thomas! Thomas!' I bellowed his name across the emptiness, running and turning, shouting, calling; my voice wavering with fear and disturbing thoughts massing in my head. There were footsteps in the snow but they led in all directions presenting no clue to his disappearance. I prayed that he had returned home even if my standing with his parents would be diminished as a result of my feeble attempts at supervision.

I shouted again, but my callings stole away into the dwindling light. Yet suddenly there was an echo cast back to me on the breeze. But it was not my voice. It was the faint laughter of a young girl. I knew she was here and my panic was now rising like an irrepressible tide.

'Where are you?' My feelings of dread shifted to anger. 'What have you done with him? Give him back.'

This time my voice rolled around the empty spaces rebounding in waves from the wall of the park keeper's hut and the houses beyond the gate, returning like the pleadings of a hundred sorry souls trapped in a perpetual nightmare.

In anguish I searched the surrounding area, clawing through the gorse and running for yards down pathways which stretched away into the dense undergrowth of the Moor. I searched for footprints, hoping I would find him hiding behind the park keeper's hut waiting to leap out, laughing at a trick well-executed. But he had vanished.

Almost in tears, I ran towards the house, terrified of finding he was not there, but intent on mustering all within its walls to scour the depths of the Moor.

Then, as I approached the gate I saw some footprints. There were mine and those of Thomas, indicating our path from the house towards the park, but beside them were two more sets. One was undoubtedly those of Thomas, as they matched exactly his footprints which stood next to my own, but next to his was another set, slightly smaller and creating a lighter impression in the snow. The footprints continued towards the side door of the house where Thomas had seemingly entered, and I prayed arrived home safely, but the second set ceased a yard or so before the door and did not continue either towards or away from the house. The snow around lay crisp, white and undisturbed.

I charged through the door and out into the garden to find Thomas and Victoria putting the finishing touches to the snowman's face using a carrot and a handful of pebbles.

Rosie emerged through the French windows with the children's coats ready to dress them for the journey home.

'So Thomas and his friend abandoned you in the park, Adam?' She smiled, wiping Thomas' hands and guiding his arms into the warmth of his brown, woollen jacket.

I was weak with relief. My head felt light, and I placed my hand against the door frame to steady myself.

'Are you all right?'

'Never finer. The running around in the park. I'm not as fit as I used to be.'

Rosie gathered Victoria and guided her back into the house. Thomas made to follow, but I placed my arm around his shoulders and led him to one side.

'Your friend, Thomas. Did you meet him in the park? Was he one of the boys next to you on the swings?'

'Oh, it wasn't a boy, Uncle Adam. It was a girl. She said she knew me and where I was from. So we walked back together.'

'What was she like?' I prayed the answer I feared would not come, but it leapt from Thomas' mouth like a demon, intent on driving a shaft of fear into my soul.

'Well, she was a bit younger than me, Uncle Adam, and she had lots of flowing, black hair and a long, raggedy cloak which was also black.'

'And did you find out her name?'

'You are trying to trick me, Uncle Adam. She said that you knew her name and that you would reveal it to me when we next met.'

He placed a piece of chocolate into his mouth, shook my hand, and ran towards his mother.

In haste I made my way to the back door in the hope that he had befriended some local child who had returned to the park, playing a childish game by placing her own steps in those already created by Thomas or myself. But as I peered out the weather had closed in and only the faintest trace of our tracks was visible beneath a new layer of smooth, white snow.

* * * * * *

'It's fortuitous that I know all the neighbours so well,' laughed Mrs Murdstone. 'It would have been Edna Baxter's daughter, Lily. About eight years old, long dark hair and keen to play pranks on the boys even at such a tender age. She'll have struck up a conversation with young Thomas and pretended she knew you. She is one for the tricks is that girl.'

'Really, I'd like to meet her.'

'Oh, there'll be little chance of that, Mr Blackwood.'

'Why is that?'

'The family left this morning. Her father has taken up a new job managing a mill in Kendal. Still, at least you'll be able to solve the mystery for young Thomas.' She paused. 'You weren't getting it into your head that Lily was the girl you saw lately in the park?'

I felt foolish. Here was another rational explanation to ease my fears and place into perspective what was becoming a mild obsession which threatened to deflect me from the real purposes of my life.

'No, no. Not at all. I am getting to know about children, I suppose. They have their own minds and love to play tricks especially if they can draw adults into their imaginary worlds.'

'That's exactly it, Mr Blackwood. Enjoy the fruits of living in Cedar Moor. Christmas is a magical time. Surround yourself with family and friends and return to work refreshed after the festivities.

She smiled at me, sympathetically. 'Now, I must get on.'

* * * * * *

That evening, I sat alone in solitary contemplation, steadfastly determined to resolve the conflict between my unexplained encounters and the plausible reasons offered by Edith Murdstone and the police officer. That they had offered advice in good faith, I had no reason to doubt. But I was a person of sound mind. I was proud of my ability to manage stressful situations. I was used to working hard, making important decisions and dealing with complicated matters. I was not the sort of person to distrust my own judgements. But now something had drifted into the edges of my life and burrowed into the foundations of my well-being. It was as if the Moor was seeing me as an interloper, someone to be left in no doubt about the power it held over those who chose to live within its presence. My experiences had echoes of the old tales which I had so casually dismissed. If my encounters were real, I could not believe I was the sole recipient of such mischief.

On my daily journeys across the Moor, I had often seen an old man, sitting alone on a bench gazing out across the green expanses. He smoked a pipe, savouring each puff and allowing the smoke to drift lazily into the air and away in the direction of his thoughts. He had the air of a man who had lived on the Moor for many years, perhaps someone who knew the difference between reality and rumour. I had nodded to him occasionally in unspoken greeting at the beginning or end of my day. The following afternoon he was there and I took my chance to engage him in conversation. I sat on the bench, and we exchanged pleasantries. I explained who I was and how I was interested in the Moor given that the village would likely become my home for several years.

His name was Luke and he had lived as man and boy in Cedar Moor, at first working the agricultural land as a shepherd and in his later years as a labourer at the cotton mill.

'They say the Moor gives up spirits.'

'Aye, that's right enough.'

'I've heard some of the stories, but I took them to be tales made up to romanticise the place.'

He turned and looked me in the eye.

'There's no romance about this place, sir. They need to be left alone, not sought after as part of any game or ghost hunt.'

'You must have seen them. As a shepherd, you will have worked through the night, out here alone.'

'I've seen flashes. Things out of the corner of my eye. The animals got restless. The dog barked. I tried to take no notice.'

'I suppose such apparitions could be mistaken for the children of travellers or circus people, hiding in the undergrowth, between the trees, delighting in tricking the innocent passer-by with their mysterious appearances?'

He laughed as if I had said the most outrageous thing.

'Circus People! Travellers! Gypsies! You think those sorts would come to the Moor? They never come up here. They're too feared of the place. They believe meddling with spirits brings bad luck. They wouldn't dare upset the dead by impersonating them. All this space and open fields. Why do you think they ignore it and camp away down by the river? They have the sense to back away. No, sir. You won't see no gypsies or their like around here. They stay away, and it's right they do so.'

I bade him good afternoon and made my way back to Laurel House. His words had caused a shift in my rational thinking. Although I had little previous interest in ghosts, I was aware of the popularity of Spiritualism amongst certain sections of society who held the belief that communication with the dead could be achieved after they had left their mortal bodies.

Indeed, I knew my mother had fostered an interest in such and had taken to reading some of the more popular spiritualist magazines of the day. I had listened, in passing, to the knowledgeable conversations she had with friends on the nature of psychical research. My mind sought connections. Could it be possible there were things I was unaware of in my childhood? Had my mother gone further than developing a passing interest in the things she had read about in magazines? If so, was I now burdened with a spirit who had travelled with me on my journey; a soul from the past who had previously established a connection with my family?

The notion was absurd. I had no evidence on which to base such outrageous theories and, if I had come across a spirit from the far reaches of the afterlife, I had come to no physical harm. But it was the dark, draining feelings which engulfed me when I was in its presence that made me inwardly shudder. I had to hope that if she was a child, then the mischievous element of her character would display a propensity to become quickly bored with silly games and move her attention elsewhere.

After a period of thought, I concluded that my best course of action was to record each occurrence in detail, noting the time and place, along with accurate sketches. It would build into a record of tangible evidence which would allow me to make reasoned interpretations of my experiences. An accurate chronicle would be of interest to someone educated in psychic research, should the time ever come when I needed to seek advice and guidance from one knowledgeable in such matters. In the meantime, I would wait, remain vigilant, and proceed with my life.

Chapter 7
Hattie

It is the nature of time to place things in perspective, and as Christmas came and went with no further sightings of the girl, my notebook lay discarded at the bottom of my travel case, all but forgotten. I began to feel that the appearances might have finally ended and that the spirit had moved on, perhaps bored with my lack of engagement, seeking a more rewarding bridge from the next world back into the company of the living. My mind had settled to the point where there were days when the thoughts and images relating to my experiences no longer troubled my thinking.

The preparations for our wedding gathered pace to the extent that matters pertaining to its organisation seemed to be the sole topic of family conversations. I began to reach the point where I preferred the commercial world of banking to the homely interaction with Joseph and the rest of the family. The discussions about who and who not to invite, the organisation of the wedding breakfast, the roles of the bridesmaids and page boys, the design of the wedding cake and numerous other trivial aspects of the day, began to make me wish I could take Wells' time machine and transport myself to the moments after we were man and wife and our departure, alone together, for our honeymoon.

Edinburgh was to be our destination. I knew the city well from visits to grandparents and I wanted to experience its imposing architecture, museums and galleries with Clara.

Joseph had already booked our stay at the Balmoral Hotel on Princess Street, placing all the attractions of the city within a short stroll. The views of the castle, sitting majestically on the weathered crags above Princess Street Gardens, would be magnificent. We might even find the energy to climb to the pinnacle of Scott Monument, that most fitting tribute to the man whose books had given me so many pleasurable hours.

It would be our first days alone together delighting in the joy of being husband and wife and the anticipation of our life together. It would be the perfect place to feed our intellectual curiosity and introduce us to the finer points of Scotland's social and historical past. We would return enriched with stories about the city which might even enthral the male members of the family and distract them from their perpetual obsession with finance, business and trade.

As spring sought to establish itself over the harsh winter, which weakened with the onset of brighter days, I busied myself at the bank progressively taking on more of Mr Tomkins' responsibilities thus allowing him to ease back into a more supervisory role. The junior clerks were gradually beginning to see me as the person in charge, and some of the more valued clients were asking for appointments with me by name. My confidence grew and my thinking about the future and life with the Jacksons began to lose its apprehension.

In March there was a welcome distraction from the wedding plans. Hannah delivered a letter to Laurel House, and I gazed upon the contents with absolute joy.

The Engagement of Our Daughter Grace
to Dr David Walker
Please attend a drinks reception at Elm House on Sunday
24th March at 3pm to share in our joy for Grace and David.
Mr and Mrs J. Jackson

As I held Joseph's card, I smiled. David had said nothing about his intentions to me and, despite his confidence and professional standing, had not dared say a word to anyone before securing Joseph's permission to marry Grace. Not that there was ever any possibility of rejection. Joseph now had the security that all his daughters had chosen well and could blossom independently of his own financial standing. He was approaching old age and would enjoy the thought of a settled retirement focusing only on himself and Mary.

* * * * * *

The day was bright, the shadows shortening, and around thirty guests filled the reception rooms in Elm House. The date of the wedding was announced as the 14th of September 1902 just four months after mine and Clara's. David made a short speech and then announced that subject to approval, I would be his best man. Joseph laughed and slapped me heartily on the back. There was joy and congratulations. Clara and Grace stood together looking radiant in their beauty. Across the room Hattie was withdrawn, speaking only in quiet episodes to Howard who seemed to be continually reassuring her.

I assumed that with each coming of a new marriage she was transported back to her early relationship with Howard and the thrill of imagining how their lives would develop. I let my own thoughts drift, musing about how I should feel should a similar scenario develop for myself and Clara. Although we were committed and devoted to each other, our conversations about the future invariably centred on children: how many we should plan for, what sexes we would prefer and the endless conjuring of suitable names for our imaginary offspring. I wondered about the darkness which might creep between us should we not be able to produce a family and how we would live with the silence and the sympathy from friends and relations.

I looked at Hattie, adrift from the tide of happiness which flowed around the room. I wondered if I might engage her in conversation and perhaps bring a little lightness into her world. However, before I could make my way across the room, she broke from Howard's arm and looked towards me.

Presently she joined me at the window. She seemed relieved to escape the happy clamour of the engagement celebrations and smiled, revealing a lightness of character which I had not encountered before. The rays of the spring sunshine fell across her face, and for a moment she looked younger and free of cares.

We stood and watched in silence as the children raced and scampered across the lawn. I struggled in my head for something to say that would not sound like a trivial conversation between two strangers. I was with my future sister-in-law and I felt the need to connect with her world, however difficult.

'Rosie must be proud of those two, even if they are such a handful.' I took a deep breath. 'Have you and Howard never considered children?'

Hattie looked past me into the garden. The smile on her face faded slightly, but she spoke with a clipped cheerfulness.

'Oh no, Adam. Life is far too exciting when you are young to be bothered with the burden of children. Howard and I have so many plans. We intend to travel and escape from Cedar Moor as often as we can.'

'Escape? It sounds like you feel imprisoned here.'

Hattie touched my arm. The smile had disappeared.

'Enjoy your freedom while you can, Adam. Talk to Clara. You are both young.' Her hand drifted slowly down my arm and her fingers wrapped around mine. 'Children can wait. You can enjoy some years of happiness before they arrive.'

She squeezed my hand gently and returned to Howard.

I turned my attention back to the garden. I was hesitant about engaging Thomas in conversation, not wanting to revisit his casual comments about the girl in the park and return my mind to wrangling once again with the events of my early days in Cedar Moor. Yet there was something still nagging at my desire to unravel the mystery that Edith Murdstone had so casually dismissed. I stepped out onto the fringes of the lawn, watching him race around the gardens, set in his own world of childish fantasy. Eventually, he caught sight of me and stumbled across leaving an unknown adventure behind.

'Uncle Adam. Pleased to meet you again, sir.' He held out his hand in manly greeting, and we shook vigorously cementing our relationship as equals rather than adult and child.

'And I am so pleased to meet you again, young man. I believe you have grown two inches since we last met.'

'Three inches,' he laughed and stood on his tiptoes to accentuate the point.

Despite my misgivings, I could not control my desire to uncover any further details Thomas might care to offer about his encounter with the girl. To this end, I suggested we take another walk across to the Moor where I could talk quietly to him and perhaps get a less cryptic explanation of whom he had met. Having gained permission from Rosie, we strolled out into the spring sunshine which presented the Moor in marked contrast to the cold, winter's afternoon of our first venture. I let Thomas run and have his play on the swings and roundabout before he settled next to me on the bench.

'We won't be meeting, Lily today, I'm afraid. Her family has moved to Kendal to enable her father to take up a new job.'

'Who is Lily?' Thomas munched on a chocolate bar seemingly disinterested by my remark.

'Ah, of course, she did not reveal her name to you when you walked back with her from the park just before Christmas. Well, that is who your casual companion was. It was Lily Baxter. She lived with her family just across the lawns in one of those small terraces near the farm. There, I have revealed her identity as she suggested I would.'

Thomas stopped munching and turned to look at me quizzically. 'Thank you, Uncle Adam, it is most interesting to know who you think she was but she could not have lived across the park.'

'What makes you say that?'

'I asked her where she was from, Uncle Adam, and it was definitely not from around here.'

'Oh, where did she say she was from?'

'She said, Uncle Adam, that she was from a place further than I could ever imagine, and that it was dark and cold and the days were like perpetual night.' He paused collecting his thoughts and then smiled and turned towards me. 'I looked in my geography books. I would think she might have come from Norway or Sweden where the winters are long and dark. Her face was so pale, Uncle Adam, almost deathly. I am sure I am right.'

Chapter 8
Marriage

Spring left Cedar Moor fresh and bright. The streets were canopied by strong, mature trees which turned the pathways into avenues of dappled light. The Moor was alive, bursting with the energy of children, and the memory of the winter chills had all but faded. Now there was only warmth, joy and the excitement of our wedding which was to take place in just over an hour's time.

David and I sat in The Plough. We were banished from all preparations which had become the domain of Mary and her daughters. The summer days and the absence of that bleak twilight time had shifted my thoughts away from the girl on the Moor. It had now been five months since the incident with Thomas, and I had not cared to speak of my experiences with anyone. I was wary of people sharing the view of Mrs Murdstone that the stress of work, and the preparations for the wedding, were somehow revealing a feebleness of spirit when confronted by occurrences which others could unravel through perfectly logical explanations.

Nevertheless, after two whiskies had infused me with the courage to share my thoughts, I looked David in the eye and posed a question.

'Do you believe in ghosts, spectres, spirits from the past? Those sort of things.'

David frowned. He swirled his whisky around in the glass, took a sip, and placed it on the table. 'I can't say definitely I do. Why do you ask?'

I recounted my experiences to him. The two fleeting appearances of the girl and the incidents in the park.

He laughed. 'So you have been here eight months and think you may have twice encountered an apparition? You are hardly the victim of some wretched spirit intent on driving you to the edge of insanity. There are definitely mischievous children around here who will play tricks to satisfy their own amusement and from what I know of Thomas he derives great pleasure from teasing adults. And you say there have been no incidents since the family gathering before Christmas?'

I nodded, feeling foolish and little embarrassed. David finished his whisky, rose from his chair and patted me on the shoulder.

'Look sharp. We have only twenty minutes before your bride will arrive.' We left The Plough and walked swiftly towards the tower of St Peter's Church.

We made our entry through the wrought-iron gate past a host of smiling faces. Joseph had pronounced that this was to be no small wedding but a celebration at which he wanted all his friends, family and the villagers to be present. I was struck by the numbers who offered me their good wishes, but they were mostly people I did not recognise. We hurried into the church, suddenly enveloped in its quiet sanctity, almost hearing the echoes of our breathing.

As we took our places at the front of the pews, the feeling came once more. I had a sudden sensation of the presence of death that can sometimes touch the soul in such places. I was abruptly at odds with the atmosphere of the day, pulled sharply away from the feelings of joy and expectation which moments ago had spilt like confetti from the people at the front gates.

'Wedding nerves?' David sensed my rising tension and gripped my shoulder. 'Don't worry. I have the ring. Clara will be with you soon. You're a lucky man.'

The sound of the organist picking out the first notes brought me back to the moment. There was the collective rustle of suits and dresses as the congregation rose together and I knew this was the beginning of everything I had wished and hoped for. In a haze of white, Clara arrived beside me. She smiled and whispered, 'I love you.' We turned to face the vicar, the music ended sharply, and the congregation settled into the body of the church with only an occasional cough breaking the holy silence.

'Who giveth this woman to be married to this man?'

'I do!' Joseph's voice echoed around the crevices and corners of the church. He gifted me Clara's hand which settled tightly into my own. I took a deep breath and looked beyond the vicar to the angels and children depicted in the stained glass window beyond the chancel. There was a momentary darkening of the picture as if a shadow had moved across the tableau, but my attention was swiftly drawn back to our exchange of vows, and soon we were pronounced man and wife, sealing our union with a kiss and retiring into the vestry to sign the register.

Smiling faces and whispered congratulations carried us out of the church and into the May sunshine. The bells pealed and the faces of local people, and a host of inquisitive children, beamed at us from beyond the walls and gates which marked the perimeter of the church grounds. I gazed into the clear, blue sky. The shadow which moved fleetingly across the church window could not have been caused by a cloud momentarily obscuring the sun's rays. Perhaps it had been a brief trick of the light or caused by a passing bird which for a moment placed itself in a direct line between the sun and window. But the end of the aisle faced north, and a warming sun shone down upon the congregation from a southerly direction.

Clara was the centre of attention. In her dress of white organdy and lace, the perfect background for the posy of orange blossom she clutched in her hand, she drew the family and guests into her presence. The offering of kisses and warm-hearted sentiments grew faint as the feelings of unease advanced, and an unstoppable tide of foreboding started to rise within me. She was here again.

Across the lawn, in the far reaches of the church grounds, she knelt at a gravestone. Her shape was almost perfectly formed, but she was still surrounded by the shadows that had accompanied her previous appearances. She was motionless, fixed in her attention, which seemed to be directed solely at the inscription written on the small, weathered headstone.

I turned swiftly back towards the congregation. They were all engaged in the cordial chatter that follows the hushed reverence of a wedding where guests are compelled to sit for nearly an hour in silence. I felt detached from it all as if I was looking through a misted window at some scene which bore no relevance to my immediate situation. I turned back, intent on hurrying across to the girl and for once confronting her, but she was gone.

I left the congregation and walked swiftly across the grass. As I was almost upon the gravestone, a movement towards the edge of the churchyard caught my eye. It was a woman of later middle age, a cloak wrapped loosely around her shoulders hurrying away from the area in which the gravestone was situated. I blinked and looked hard. The woman had a clear similarity to Edith Murdstone, but her movement was swift, and I could not be sure. I called after her, but she hurried away without turning. In an instant, I was standing on the spot occupied by the young girl only moments ago.

I knelt and peered at the weathered inscription on the stone face. The church was barely fifty years old, but the stone looked like it had been there for centuries. Moss and lichen clung to its face, and I scraped it away as best I could, shaking as the letters on the stone became clearly visible

SAM
BLACKWOOD
A beloved child
born.............. died 8th June 1902

I started to sweat; a cold, clammy sweat which froze out the rays of the sun which cast my shadow across the stonework. How could this be? Was it some kind of sorcery? Today was May 16th, 1901, yet I gazed at the grave of some child, yet to die, who shared my family name. I felt faint, unsteady, as I raised myself from the ground. Trying to keep my composure I turned and hurried back across the lawn, forcing my way through the congregation. I grabbed David's arm, pulling him away from his conversation with Grace and half dragged him in the direction of the gravestone.

'Steady, man.' David released my grip, turned and made some signal back towards the guests whose attention was now directed away from Clara, watching in concern as I trod a wavering path back across the lawn with David shouting questions at me for which I had no answer.

I reached the spot where moments before I had gazed at the weathered stone with the bewildering inscription. The grass was flat, empty, perfectly manicured and untouched.

'There was a grave here!' I blurted to David, almost on the verge of tears. 'It was the grave of, of...' I grasped the name from the air based on my memory of the letters. 'Sam! I'm sure it was...Sam Blackwood. It was being tended by the young girl dressed in black. He dies on the 8th of June 1902.'

David gazed disbelievingly at me, and I realised the absurdity of what I was saying.

'Keep calm, man. Joseph will have you committed to a sanatorium if you repeat what you have just said to me. Come quickly. You need a moment to recover.'

Without looking back, we walked away from the congregation and moved out of sight behind the church.

'This is the girl you were talking about in The Plough?'

'It was her.'

'What were you thinking about before she appeared?'

'You know that. My life together with Clara. The joy and happiness of us being together.'

'And the times before?'

I thought carefully. 'Arriving to take up my job in Cedar Moor and being with Clara. The joy of Joseph finally agreeing to our engagement. The excitement of a family Christmas. Why? What are you thinking?'

'That those thoughts may well be the key, Adam. Although they are joyous, they mask your deep-rooted anxieties. Your worries about being accepted into a rich and prominent family and being able to provide for Clara. It seems to me that she comes to you whenever anxieties about your life with Clara dominate your thoughts.'

'Are you saying these things are not real?'

'I believe anxiety can cause a heightened awareness of your senses. Thinking you heard something. Catching movement out of the corner of your eye. Feeling that something touches you. These can be symptoms created by a nervous disorder. Come, let us rejoin the celebrations.'

'But I clearly saw a gravestone with the name of a child yet to die.'

He ignored me, and we moved around the side of the church. David purposefully strode ahead towards the waiting congregation.

'No need to panic everyone. Adam was certain he had seen a suspicious character lurking in the shadows behind the church. We have checked the grounds, and all is well. Let us all enjoy the celebrations for this is indeed a day to cherish and remember.'

He guided me up the path towards the carriage which was waiting to take us to Dunsbury Hall. He spoke quietly to me as Clara approached on Joseph's arm. 'Let us keep our thoughts to ourselves. I am no doctor of madness, but you may need to learn how to cast doubt upon your own perceptions. See me at my surgery on your return from Edinburgh, and we can talk this through.'

Clara arrived by my side, and we climbed together into the carriage to begin our journey together. We sped down Cedar Moor Road through the lines of well-wishers, but I could not speak. Time seemed to slow and sound drifted to the periphery of my senses but as we arrived at Dunsbury Hall I had managed to partially recover and taking a handkerchief from my suit pocket I wiped a tear of happiness from Clara's face.

'I want this to be the start of a wonderful life together.'

A smile crossed her face, and she took me in her arms.

'You look tired, Adam. Everything seems to have happened so quickly. When we reach Edinburgh we will be able to rest, explore the sites and enjoy the freshness of the air. There will just be the two of us. We will delight in the pleasure of being alone.'

.

Chapter 9
Edinburgh

Late the next day Clara and I waited on the bustling platform of Manchester's Victoria Station. Here were people arriving from their day's business, completing short journeys from local stations or from across the Pennines, others climbing from great express trains that had made the long haul from London or Newcastle. We were lost in the confusion of it all. A porter guided us to Platform 7 where attendants swarmed around the carriages loading food, bedding, clean plates and cutlery into the coaches which shone red and cream against the grey iron stanchions of the concourse.

As the train thundered through the night, I gazed into the darkness. Here I was, my beloved Clara resting her head on my shoulders, the rumble of the carriages lulling her into a deep and contented sleep. But there was no such space in my head in which the thoughts of the last few months might be suppressed and disappear.

David's sceptical reaction to my revelations about the girl was not unexpected coming from a man of medical and scientific knowledge. But there was no rational explanation this time. No way in which I could explain the appearance and disappearance of the grave by some trick of the light or anxiety-driven hallucination. Her appearance had been forewarned. I had felt her in the church, sensed her presence as the fleeting shadow was cast across the stained glass window. There had been the same draining of happiness and contentment that had first occurred when I alighted from the train at Cedar Moor.

Now I decided, it was time to confide in Clara and offer her the real explanation for my behaviour at the wedding, and the details of my subsequent conversation with David.

I moved her head gently from my shoulders and allowed her time to fully awaken before embarking on an account of the events. She listened, the initial smile on her face fading as my story unfolded. I could sense the realisation rising within her that I carried with me a set of beliefs which any sane person would find absurd. As I reached the point of revealing the name Sam Blackwood, and the date of his predicted death, a tear fell from her eye and she grasped my hand firmly as the train sped on.

'This is inconceivable, Adam. You must know it is impossible. The appearances of the girl to you must be a coincidence: an urchin as people have suggested. Young Thomas is prone to the wild bouts of imagination characteristic of a boy of his years. He would have known the name of the girl in the park. He was teasing you; can't you see?'

'And the grave?' The fleeting anger I had felt at David's response rose again within me. Clara did not believe me, but in a moment I was filled with regret at revealing my thoughts and subjecting her to the worry and panic reflected in her gaze. I decided not to continue.

'You are right. You must think me an idiot. The stress of the wedding distracted my thoughts in a way I could never have thought possible. The sun was strong and the heat and commotion of the day must have got the better of me. David has suggested a consultation on my return.'

'Clara wiped away the tear and smiled. 'It was exactly that, Adam. You need to put those events behind you. You must trust in David. You need to relax and free your mind from worry. When we return your resolve will be strengthened. We will have excellent stories to tell of our week in a wonderful city.'

The train sped northwards. Clara rested against me, but I realised I was alone. As I settled for the night, I prayed that our time in Edinburgh would somehow release me from the anguish of trying to find reason in the events and that on our return to Cedar Moor my connection with the girl, or whatever she might represent, would be broken.

Nevertheless, from the moment I had gazed upon the gravestone, I felt disconnected from the world around me. At our wedding reception, Clara and I had been the focus of everyone's attention, but I felt invisible, discarded, unwanted. My mind was a source of endless wandering, a journey along a path without any direction. My heart should have been bursting with an explosion of emotion, but it was constricted by fear and anxiety. The train hurtled on. In a few hours, it would leave the darkness behind and emerge into the light of a new day. I prayed I could do the same. I closed my eyes and was drawn to sleep by the steady rhythm of the speeding locomotive.

* * * * * *

I had to clear my mind of the girl on the Moor. I forced myself to believe that the respite from the source of my preoccupation might loosen its hold on my thoughts and allow me to return to a more reasoned state of mind. When I returned, I should view Cedar Moor afresh as if it were my first visit to the village. I would rid myself of dark thoughts, channel my energies into work at the bank and treat the start of my life with Clara as a new beginning. Should I be confronted with the girl again, I would simply walk away adopting an unconcerned approach. I would convince myself that she was without earthly substance and that my mind was mischievously trying to transport me back to those days of childhood fantasy. Edinburgh would be the perfect place to cultivate my new resolve.

The first few days afforded me a welcome degree of relaxation. It was an exciting city, in many ways similar to Manchester but with a cultural heart that drew us to several of its excellent galleries and museums. The Balmoral sat at the head of Princess Street and our evenings were spent walking in the gardens in the shadow of its ancient castle.

'Greyfriars Bobby,' said Clara one evening. 'I should like to see the statue. It is such a sad story.'

We climbed the hill to the Royal Mile and continued along George IV Bridge. Presently, we reached the statue which was surrounded by a mass of tourists.

'It is so busy here!' exclaimed Clara. 'May we go and find the actual graves of the poor dog and his master? I believe they are in the graveyard over there.'

Through a small alleyway behind the statue was the entrance to Greyfriars Kirk and its churchyard. It was late afternoon, and patches of light rested amongst the pathways and trees. The dark stones leaned tiredly as if years in memoriam had gradually sapped their resolve to remain upright. Huge monuments and tombs towered above more humble stones and crosses but almost all were weathered and worn. Not a flower or card of remembrance was to be seen. It was as if all who lay beneath the graves had been buried long ago, lying forgotten, abandoned, left to spend eternity in the dank, grey earth.

Clara walked ahead of me towards the graves of the night-watchman, John Gray, and his faithful dog, Bobby, who remained at the side of his master's grave for fourteen years after his death.

'Poor thing,' she sighed. 'Such devotion, yet he was still placed to rest in unconsecrated ground, with just a stone as a mark of remembrance. He deserves a proper place to rest in the company of God. I hope, for his sake, he is not wandering like a lost spirit with the same restlessness he showed in life.'

She took a handkerchief from her bag and caught a tear which fell from her eye. I thought it poignant that she should be so moved by the plight of the poor animal, but then I noticed that her gaze fell beyond Bobby's stone to a patch of ground close to the wall of the churchyard which sheltered a row of newer, smaller gravestones.

Her eyes fixed momentarily on the spot before she turned away.

'I shall go and seek out the grave of his master now.' She spoke indirectly as if her words were thoughts and not intended for my hearing. I thought I could discern a slight waver in her voice before she turned quickly and moved on.

I began to feel uneasy, with the memory of my experiences in St Peter's churchyard less than a week ago still present despite my resolution to cast them to the back of my mind. With every flickering movement of light and the appearance and disappearance of visitors behind the huge tombstones that dominated some of the burial plots, I began to feel apprehensive and vulnerable.

The area between the dog's grave and the line of newer plots was overgrown, the weeds, roots, mounds of dead leaves and rotting vegetation creating a barrier to my inquisitive nature. The last vestiges of sunlight flickered weakly between the trees and headstones and a stray shaft of light cast my shadow across Bobby's stone and the graves which lay beyond.

And then a presence crept upon me. From the corner of my eye, I perceived that I had been silently joined by a young girl. As her shadow moved next to mine, we stood as dark accomplices reaching towards the stone.

I spun around but the pathway was empty, and there were no footprints to match my own in the light covering of soil that surrounded the stone. I turned back swiftly. The shadow had disappeared. The wind whipped up, and flecks of shade spread across the churchyard wall and the nearby gravestones. But I was in no doubt about what I had seen. It had been no misconception. The shadow I had glimpsed was perfectly formed, unmoving within a companionable distance to my own. I felt a rising panic and suddenly a shape seemed to dart and weave between the towering tombstones. As my eyes strove to follow it I became dizzy and stumbled, losing my balance and tumbling to the ground.

I sat on the dry earth, breathing deeply, looking for signs of movement between the gravestones but what shadows there were stretched flat and unmoving between the tombs

I placed my hand on the top of Bobby's stone. The summer air was warm but the stone was as cold as death. Then came the laughter. Not an audible sound but one that pierced my senses and sat momentarily inside my head before being ripped away to nothingness in the heavy air.

I pulled myself from the earth and wiped away the soil and dead leaves from my jacket and trousers. For a moment I struggled for my bearings not knowing which way Clara had gone and my confusion turned into sudden anxiety that I may never see her again. I ran down the gravelled path towards the entrance to the Kirk arriving at the gate with my heart beating wildly as I grasped the rusting metal for support. Then she was with me, holding my arm, brushing away the last of the marks from my jacket and trousers with her white gloves.

82

'Adam, what has happened?' She had a motherly tone in her voice and looked at me with some concern. 'You look worried. Is everything all right?'

'Never better. I tripped on some dry roots. I am annoyed at my clumsiness.'

She smiled and we moved on away from the crowds and back to the Balmoral. I dared not reveal the incidents of my ordeal to her. I had to protect her from something which was either emanating from the menacing world of the paranormal or from within the desolate reaches of my mind.

Back in the hotel room, I once again tried to rationalise what I had experienced. The shadow could conceivably have been cast by a nearby tree moving in the wind and removing the shape from my side as quickly as it had been presented. The laughter in my head conceivably a result of my dizziness and panic.

I wanted to believe that all the appearances and unexplained happenings might somehow have the plausible explanations to which others had alluded. But it was the appearance of the grave at St Peter's which troubled me; the perplexing mystery of Sam Blackwood, the boy bearing my family name who seemingly had just over a year to live on this earth. If it were some kind of hallucination then I could succumb to David's theory that I was suffering from temporary mental fatigue which would produce such symptoms until the source of my affliction was resolved. I wanted to believe this was the case and that a simple period of rest would prove a welcome cure, but I felt healthy and alert, lacking no amount of energy or burdened with debilitating thoughts about work or my life with Clara.

I felt the need to be more earnest of spirit, to throw my energies into connecting the pieces of the puzzle that were detailed in the small notebook which had travelled with me.

If the girl and the gravestone were to appear again, I needed to know if, as an earthy mortal, I could make contact and find some comforting reason as to why I was suddenly the focal point of a force beyond my comprehension.

It was to this end that I found myself in the Edinburgh Central Library on North Bridge Street. I had left Clara to enjoy a couple of hour's shopping and made my way through the stone-arched entrance into the quiet echoes of the reception hall. The assistant looked at me curiously when I enquired as to whether they had a section on the occult, perhaps concluding that I was some casual devil worshipper who had headed north to seek a land of desolate reaches and impious tales. She directed me to a small room on the third floor where a young man sat pouring over a large book full of maps, ancient writings and religious symbols.

He was of a similar age to myself, dressed smartly in a tweed suit, white linen shirt, and a neatly arranged cravat of floral design.

He seemed to have that slight air of eccentricity characteristic of those absorbed in the pursuit of academic knowledge. He held the book closely as if the small, round spectacles he wore lacked the power to allow him to read from a reasonable distance. His nose hovered only an inch from the page, and his finger traced the words slowly and meticulously along each line. For a few moments, I sat and watched him. He seemed oblivious to my presence and constantly muttered to himself, posing questions and ideas which, within a matter of moments, had been answered or had become the focus of counter-questions batted to and fro from one muttering to the next.

As the knowledge journeyed from the page into his mind, the mutterings continued, interrupted only to allow himself to scribble words or symbols into a small, leather-bound notebook.

He appeared to be immersed in the prescient examination of worlds beyond our own. Despite being strangers, I elected to engage him in conservation with the hope that the answers I might be seeking could already lie within his sphere of knowledge.

I introduced myself, and we immediately seemed to strike up a bond of friendship. His name was Andrew Donne, a student of theology at the university. I asked him if he might have some interest in my experiences of the past few months.

He listened intently as I outlined my story before closing his books thoughtfully and retrieving a small volume of work from a nearby shelf. He opened the book carefully and turned to one of the middle chapters.

'We may find some answers in here, sir. *Spirits of the Age. A Study In Contemporary Supernatural Phenomena* by A R Campbell Brown. It is the definitive work on current supernatural theories. Mr Campbell Brown was my former tutor at Edinburgh University until his untimely death by,..' He paused. 'Well, enough of that. Suffice to say he is at peace with his work. Let us move on.'

He directed my attention back to the book which lay open before me.

'It seems to me, sir, that you have stumbled into the presence of a shadow person. See here. They are well-documented across time. It would match your experiences. They are normally seen in the corner of the eye, pass by quickly, and then disappear. They often stand in doorways or corners watching their victims.'

'Victims?' He recognised the alarm caused by his comment and his tone softened, moving from that of an academic lecturer to one of a concerned confidante intent on delivering a warning to someone who might be in peril.

'What you describe is unusual. Shadow people do not usually appear in such substantial form as detailed by your experience of the child at the grave. It appears that the spirit you describe can move from the shadow world and connect with the living present. I believe Mr Campbell Brown had some experience with such entities during the writing of his book. It may be worth you reading this chapter in detail if your time in Edinburgh allows.'

He returned to his chair and placed one hand across his forehead as if any further advice required a degree of deep concentration and thought. He took a pen and paper from his briefcase and scribbled quickly upon the blank page.

'My address, sir, and you must give me yours. We must keep close contact. It is my plan to continue my studies at the Theologian College in Manchester. I am presently awaiting confirmation of my place.' He pushed back in his chair and lifted his eyes in the direction of the ceiling.

'I have come across such incidents before where a spirit placed itself within the domain of a mortal being.' He looked down and turned towards me. 'I must tell you that the outcomes are not always agreeable.'

'Is there anything I can do?'

'I do not wish to cause you alarm, but a spirit which clings desperately to a life which is lost may be exhibiting a degree of malevolence. I would be aware. If it does have the intention to do you harm, then you should search into your past to see if you can find any connection with its former life.'

'And if I do find such a thing?'

'Then you will need to somehow make your peace.' He turned and looked out at the drab Edinburgh sky as if deliberately avoiding my gaze. 'I hope it is something you manage to achieve.'

* * * * * *

The remainder of our week went quickly, our trips to the Edinburgh Castle and Roslyn Chapel passing without incident. I had managed to secure a couple of spare hours to return to the library and delve into Mr Campbell Brown's book. Andrew's observations were confirmed. If the girl was indeed a shadow person, then it was likely that she was seeking a release from this world to enable her to move into the spiritual calm of the next. Something, however, would be causing her to cling to her previous life. Something that needed to be resolved before she could be released from her twilight existence and leave the mortal pain behind. It would seem that I was a bridge to some event of which I was, as yet, unaware.

I was determined that, on our return to Cedar Moor, I would address the mystery of the grave of Sam Blackwood with some vigour. I assumed that the girl was in some way connected to Sam; either a spirit of the future, who was appearing to me with the intent of averting his untimely death or a distant relative from the past with the ability to peer into the future to pre-warn me of his impending doom.

This would be my starting point. I would explore the family history, delving into all available records of the Blackwood line with the hope that some clue might suddenly emerge and the appearances of the girl would be given a plausible explanation.

Chapter 10
Rosie

After returning from Edinburgh, we settled into our rooms at Elm House. The villa had been built to accommodate the large family that Joseph had planned. In addition, there were servants quarters, mostly unused now as the need for service staff had decreased as the children grew and left home. We were given an annexe towards the rear of the house with its own bedroom, sitting room, kitchen and a portion of private garden.

I had two days leave remaining before I was required to return to my duties at the bank. Clara planned to spend most of this time on shopping trips with her mother, acquiring certain items of furniture and decorative oddments which would allow us to feel homely in our portion of the property.

I decided to use this time to explore my family history and the details of all birth, deaths, and marriages for as far back as I could trace, in the hope of finding a connection with the child, Sam Blackwood and the girl. Perhaps I could trace some family tragedy involving a child which would produce a credible connection with her, together with a possible explanation as to why she desired to connect with my earthly existence.

On the pretence of meeting an old friend for lunch, I made my way to Manchester Town Hall and the records office for births, deaths and marriages. After a brief explanation of my intentions, the registrar directed me into a small reading room and presently arrived with some sizeable files stamped with the title 'Parish of Bolton', and the local census records for the previous century.

'The parish registers are your best bet. You'll find records here dating back to before 1800. The censuses will only take you back to 1837. Your surname is not too common so you should have some chance of success.'

I was left alone. It did not take me long to find the wedding certificate relating to my mother and father and the record of my own birth, on the 7th June 1877, some two years after their marriage. After that, there was the birth certificate of my younger sister and various records of cousins, aunts and uncles: all of whom I was fully aware. The morning was ebbing away along with my sense of purpose. I sensed that perhaps I was wasting my time and that, this child, if she was a spirit, would be looking down on me and revelling in my foolishness.

I decided to have some lunch after which I would check the census records in the hope I might untangle the web of ancestry and find a link between Sam, myself and the girl. However, on my return, I quickly found boredom and frustration were beginning to sap my desire to delve any further into the volumes of records which stretched out across the table. I tidied them back into order and informed the clerk that my search was complete even though it had failed to reveal any threads which might connect the appearance of the girl with my own family history.

'Would you like to browse our newspaper archives, sir?'

I had not considered these as a source of evidence which I realised was quite foolish of me. However, I was sceptical that they would direct me to anything which might suddenly throw light upon the mystery. Still, I would spend the time with a dual purpose and perhaps gain a better insight into the life and history of Cedar Moor. The girl could possibly be a local child, and I had little sense of Clara's family history. It would be of some interest to gain an insight into Joseph and

Mary's life at around the time they had Rosie, their first child. If the newspaper cuttings threw up any sort of clue as to the girl, it would provide an unexpected profit from my day's toils.

'Thank you. I'm interested in the area of Cedar Moor near Stanport.'

'As far as I am aware, sir, Cedar Moor and Stanport have no daily newspapers of their own. The Stanport Chronicle, a fortnightly publication, would probably contain references to that area. What period are you specifically interested in?'

'Perhaps the editions from around the 1870s.' I made a quick calculation of the likely year of the girl's death if she had met her end recently. 'And those of 1892 to 1894.'

The clerk led me down to the basement which smelled of stale air and damp paper. Along the side wall of a large chamber were volumes of newspapers. At the far end on the lower shelves were files named 'Stanport Chronical'. There seemed to be around sixty in all, each file containing twenty-six editions from a particular year. They presented an overwhelming amount of information and history, and I was at a loss to know where to begin.

I had around two hours to explore the periods of interest and then I would need to return to Elm House before a degree of worry set into Clara's mind. The editions from the early 1890s threw up no records of the disappearance or death of a child of comparable age so, with time slipping away, I elected to browse through the first year of the 1870s. I heaved the volume up onto the desk, wiped the dust from its surface with my sleeve, and lifted the heavy cloth cover.

The first few editions from 1870 were of no interest, for little happens in such a town after the excitement and revelry of Christmas and the New Year celebrations. The news from the area for the early months was predictable with articles on the inclement weather, coping with heavy snowfall, and advice on how to treat seasonal ailments. There was a heart-warming story of a dog rescued from Stanport Viaduct and, given the nature of the season, numerous adverts for funeral directors. I quickly skimmed through to April, leaving winter behind.

I was about to return the volume to its place on the shelf when an article relating to Cedar Moor caught my attention. It was in large print and seemed to be the biggest story of the year to date:

Local Financier Lost In Drowning Tragedy.

I read on. It was a tragic story of a young local investment banker, Stephen Derbyshire, who had gone fishing with some friends on Tatton Mere. When they were in the middle of the lake, a ferocious storm swept out of nowhere, and the force of the rain was enough to overwhelm and capsize the boat. His two companions managed to swim to the shore and raise the alarm but Stephen was a poor swimmer and by the time help arrived he had disappeared. His body was recovered some hours later from the northern edge of the lake.

I felt pity for the man for losing his young life in such unfortunate circumstances. I was about to close the file when the last line, at the bottom of the page, caused me to pause.

'Stephen is survived by his wife, Mary, and his daughter, Rosie, of three months.'

This had to be some wild coincidence but when I turned the page the continuation of the story cast my mind into a state of confusion.

Joseph Jackson, a local property investor, paid tribute to his close friend stating that he was the most likeable of gentlemen and that all must be done to support his family through their unfortunate loss.'

I slammed the book shut and climbed the stairs rapidly, entering the records office at a pace which took the clerk by surprise.

'Give me the records of marriages for Stanport for the years 1870 to 1872. Hurry, please!'

In a few minutes, the clerk returned carrying three large volumes, breathing heavily and sweating under their weight. I grabbed each one from him and laid them out across the desk. In a matter of moments, my thoughts of coincidence had been banished. Joseph had married Mary Derbyshire on the 15th April 1871 less than a year after the tragedy. Rosie was not his child.

I sat thinking as the train to Cedar Moor rattled its way through the outskirts of the city. I had little idea what I was to make of this new knowledge, or indeed whether it was any of my business. There were, however, unanswered questions which gripped me. Why had I not been informed of this considerable piece of family history? Were the other three sisters aware that Rosie was a step-sister? Then again, I reasoned to myself, what difference would the passing of this knowledge make. It was probably best left unsaid. Rosie herself might have no knowledge of her real father, being only three months old at the time of the tragedy and far too young to have any recollection of a wedding. Within the Jackson household, Rosie's position was as much established as that of her sisters. She was the one the younger girls looked up to for guidance. She was invariably the voice of sense and reason in moments when decisions had to be made and conflicts resolved.

I decided it was not my place to say anything or delve further into the matter. It would have to be another piece of information that I would keep locked inside my head, constricting the space that should have been filled with happiness and contentment. I wanted to empty my mind, wash away the confusion that pulled my thinking down first one avenue and then the next, each one encountering a dead end of worry and uncertainty. Everyone around me was happy and living in joyous anticipation of the future. I was sinking, and I had no one within my circle of family and friends who might support me through darker hours which were becoming more frequent as time crept on.

.

Chapter 11
Deterioration

Over the next few days, the knowledge of Rosie's parentage was replaced in my thoughts by the frustrations of not being able to establish any connection between my own life, past or present, Sam Blackwood, or the restless spirit. Further investigations of news articles had revealed nothing, and I was approaching the point of some despair. I now had new knowledge in my possession to add to the mystery of the girl, and worry and anxiety fed my mind through each working day. I had no one with whom to discuss my fear. Not just the fear of the girl, whoever or whatever she may be, but also a fear for my own sanity.

I constantly tried to look into the future to try and imagine a final scenario which would revolve around the 8th of June 1902. I wanted to believe that it would be the end. I imagined it would be the date on which everything would return to normal, and the girl would disappear, whether the fate of Sam Blackwood had been resolved or not. But I fretted about the time beyond, time stretching into those days yet to be lived. Not long ago my life had been simple, focused, a model of health and happiness. Now it was dark, suffocating, my every moment taken by thoughts which grew more anxious each day. I was becoming consumed by worries which could not be shared with anyone lest I be labelled a creature of irrational thought driven by an uncontrollable obsession.

My only hope was to talk to Andrew. I had written to him twice, but each time the letter had been returned marked 'Address Unknown'. I had contacted the Theologian College who told me he had declined his place and that they had had no further contact with him. As the days passed, I waited. I waited for her to come once more.

I found it difficult to concentrate on anything else, believing that in all probability my ordeal would continue. I felt anxious and on edge, waiting for the next appearance, overreacting to every shifting of the light and drifting of the evening shadows. I felt as if I was living on a precipice, on the one hand clinging to the normality of life but on the other peering into the dark unknown which somehow would inevitably have to be visited and explored. Against this towering monster of fear, I tried to maintain an outward calm to all who knew me.

However, as the days wore on my mental strength began to drain, and my sleep was characterised by spasms of fear and episodes of fitful nightmares.

And then in the depth of a dream she came to me. There was water swirling and suffocating. Grass and undergrowth growing, wrapping roots around me, tightening, constricting my breathing and in the midst was a hand, reaching, beckoning almost within my grasp. Then, from within the confusion came the cry, 'Help me! Help me!' before the twisting, tumbling vision swept a torrent of fear so terrifying that I awoke, my clothes soaked, and my eyes fixed on some indistinguishable point across the room.

Clara was at my side, holding me tightly in an attempt to arrest the trembling that was causing my body to shake with such force that the stout, wooden bed frame creaked and groaned.

She brought me a flannel, pressing it to my brow, providing a moment of welcome calm. I breathed steadily and noticed my heartbeat beginning to drop. I sat on the side of the bed holding my head unsteadily in my quivering hands.

'You must make an appointment to see David. These troublesome ruminations of your mind can be cured, Adam. It is not only myself who is aware of the deterioration of your spirit. People are making upsetting comments within my presence, whispered asides designed to catch my attention which I cannot help but notice. You have not been yourself for some weeks.'

Clara was right. At work, I had been conscious for days that all eyes in the office had been upon me. Instead of the automatic passing of transactions, the junior clerks examined every ledger entry and piece of documentation that passed through their hands. I had no doubt this was a missive from Mr Tomkins who watched me steadily as I worked on my accounts. His insistence on promoting a positive image for the bank was becoming undermined by my appearance. My eyes were sunken and tired and my face sometimes only half-shaven. My general demeanour presented that of a man who was not taking care of his appearance and I had lost my zest for work, undertaking my tasks in a languid state conversing with clients in a monotonous tone.

Things came to a head on the last Friday in June. My tiredness was such that I inadvertently transferred £20 of the bank's money into the account of a local publican, Arthur Jeffries. He had paid £2 into his account, but in my state of tiredness and anxiety, I had added an extra nought in the ledger. The new balance of the account was relayed to Jeffries who was not a pleasant man. When I called him into the office to explain the error, he insisted that the transaction stand and that his solicitor would be making the case known to head office.

For days I could not sleep. There had been no more physical appearances of the girl, but she was inside my mind, shifting all other thoughts with such determination that I found it impossible to concentrate on the most simple of tasks. My feeble attempts to banish her from my conscience floundered in the images delivered with the night. I craved some potion or sleeping draught which would deliver rest, but I feared it would move me into a deeper state of slumber with no escape from the distressing, clawing dreams.

In desperation, I visited David at his surgery in Cedar Moor. He listened intently as I outlined the deterioration of my health. He examined me thoroughly checking the beating of my heart and listening to my breathing, before sitting me down and giving his diagnosis.

He talked at some length, outlining his opinion on my mental state, preferring to assert that it was my work, education and general intelligence that had made me susceptible to over-thinking and illogical reaction towards perfectly plausible situations. He even put forward the theory that the increase in such disorders of the mind was the result of an evolutionary process and that brain workers from the educated classes were particularly vulnerable.

His theories were partly reassuring, as was his belief that people suffering from disorders of the mind could still lead an active life within society provided they came to terms with their condition and accepted its limitations. I listened, but his words failed to turn me to the belief that everything encountered was the result of an overactive mind. I had displayed no such symptoms until I arrived in Cedar Moor, and I had the scholarly insight of Andrew Donne who immediately accepted my encounters with the unexplained as perfectly believable happenings. Whatever David's belief, he chose not to burden me with a formal diagnosis that I was suffering from a mental illness.

'In my opinion, Adam, you are undoubtedly suffering from nervous exhaustion, and we need to do something otherwise your mind will be tipped over the edge, and your world will fall irretrievably apart. I will write a letter to the bank explaining that my medical judgement is that you are suffering from a mild and temporary attack of nerves brought on by the excessive demands of work; as I previously mentioned, not uncommon amongst those with such responsibilities. I suggest rest and recuperation as a treatment. Spend the time between now and Christmas away from the pressures of work. It will give you time to find yourself again and put this obsession with the supernatural behind you.'

He came around the table and gripped my hand.

'It is likely she is not real, Adam. You need to believe that. She is undoubtedly emanating from the misconceptions of your mind. You must suppress your thoughts and concentrate on your family. They are the real world, and they are your responsibility.'

'I thought there was a possibility you might believe me.'

'Adam, I am firstly a man of medicine and science. My training tells me that there is a logical, scientific explanation for all that happens on this earth. I studied for a few months in Germany before graduating. They have a word for what I believe may be the cause of your unrest. They term it neurosis. It is a relatively mild mental condition that is not caused by organic disease. Symptoms of stress, anxiety, obsessive behaviour and irrational thoughts are common characteristics. Try not to worry. It is not a radical loss of touch with reality and something from which you can make a full recovery.'

He spoke clearly and calmly to me. 'Adam, I have seen many people die, but none resurrected back to life. Everything about my studies and training tells me it is not possible. However,..'

He paused as if trying to choose his words carefully before he continued.

'..I am a man of religious beliefs. Although I have no evidence of an afterlife, I cannot eliminate the possibility from my thinking. It is just that I have never come across any evidence. But I can offer you friendship and support. I will not abandon you or dismiss you as some obsessive crank.'

He placed his hand on my shoulder and returned to his desk where he wrote quickly on a piece of official-looking paper.

'Take this to Charles Tomkins and ask him to contact head office. They will take note of my diagnosis.'

He folded the letter, sealed it shut and handed it to me.

'You must draw on your inner strength, Adam. All will be well. Take time to reassure yourself and look to your family.'

* * * * * *

The next day I arrived at the bank early. As was his routine, Mr Tomkins was already in his office perusing the day's appointments. He looked surprised to see me but also relieved when I outlined the details of my appointment with David and presented him with the letter. In less than an hour, I was on my way home. Mr Tomkins was a man of influence in banking circles and had telephoned head office who accepted his recommendation that I should have some months unpaid leave. A replacement clerk was already on the way to take over my duties. All being well, I would be able to return refreshed, and 'reborn' as Mr Tomkins put it. He shook my hand, gripped me around the shoulders and wished me a speedy recovery.

Chapter 12
Alice

Clara was pleased. She saw it as an opportunity for me to focus on recovering my well-being without the distractions of work. For my part, I was worried. I could not envisage how I might fill up the days which now stretched before me without the focus and routines of my job.

After a week of relaxing in the garden, reading and concentrating on emptying my mind, a restless, nervousness began to grip me and I craved something to fill the long hours.

Unsurprisingly, it was Joseph who dictated my direction. He had strong connections with the Church in Stanport, Cedar Moor and in Dunsbury. They were always in need of volunteers to help with the upkeep of the grounds and minor renovations to the fabric of their buildings. He would put me in contact with the Reverend Powell at St Mary's who oversaw the affairs of two local churches and one in Dunsbury. He was in no doubt that a spell of physical work would improve the state of my mind and that some painting, carpentry and gardening would secure a good supply of oxygen to the brain and commence the healing process.

I had little choice. As the hot summer days bathed Cedar Moor in a constant glow of gold, I swapped my smart work suit for the attire of a working tradesman and turned my hand to whatever work the Reverend Powell could find for me.

The majority was within the grounds of each church, clearing pathways, extricating weeds and stretches of rampant foliage that had claimed parts of the lawns and flower beds as their own. There was a regular supply of sanding, varnishing and small masonry jobs which fell within my ability, despite my lack of professional skills and experience. The work proved tiring, but it contributed to nights of welcome sleep on days when I would arrive back at Elm House exhausted.

At the end of my first month, I was told that some urgent work was needed at St Martin's Church in Dunsbury. Its congregation was sparse, and a general lack of money had caused the church grounds to fall into a ragged state. A new vicar was due to arrive, and it would be appropriate if all were as tidy as possible when he took up his position. There would be a good two weeks of work for me to undertake with the added bonus that my journey to work would be a pleasant stroll along the River Mersey. The Reverend Powell assured me that the soothing sound of the swirls and eddies around its banks would ensure that I arrived home each evening relaxed after my day's exertions.

I had my reservations about spending long hours alone. I talked with Clara about my concerns regarding the isolated nature of the work and my worry that keeping my own company would lead to brooding and unwelcome thoughts. She was comforting, convincing me that there was a daily improvement in my condition and that my normal state of mind was beginning to reassert itself. She assured me that each day she could sense the change in my nature. I seemed calmer, happier and less prone to falling into low spirits. My change of character had lightened her spirit, and she knew just the thing that would settle me in my new task. Whatever this might be remained unannounced. I would have to wait a few days before her strategy could be revealed.

The day before I was to start my voluntary work at St Martin's, Clara met me at the gate of Elm House and ushered me into the morning room.

'Adam, close your eyes.'

I did as I was bid and was led out into the garden. There on the lawn stood Hannah holding firmly onto a lead that restrained a black and white springer spaniel who pulled towards me as if in greeting.

I smiled. 'Is this an addition to our family or is he on a casual visit?'

'He is for you,' beamed Clara. 'He will be your friend and companion while you are out on your daily tasks. He will be someone to talk to should you feel lonely and despondent and David says that pets are a blessing to help divert a person's worries and anxieties.'

I walked across to the dog. His bright eyes shone in anticipation and he put out his paw as if in greeting. I took it and stroked him for a few moments, and the excessive wagging of his tale seemed to indicate we had formed an instant friendship. Hannah released him from the lead, and he followed me obediently around the garden sitting at my command and walking to heel as if he knew his purpose as man's best friend.

'Isn't he wonderful?' said Clara. 'I acquired him from Mr and Mrs Bramwell at Laurel Bank Farm. He is two years old and already well-trained. He will be your friend and guide in the days to come.'

The dog seemed like the perfect solution to my worries. He was called Max, a good strong name which I liked immensely, and saw no reason to change it lest it confuse the poor animal. I took an instant belief that the comforting presence of my new friend would hasten my recovery and that my life would soon return to normal.

The following morning, we set out together for Dunsbury. In my bag I had my sandwiches, fruit and water, and for Max some meaty scraps Hannah had saved from the previous evening's meal. The walk from Cedar Moor to Dunsbury was just short of two miles, most of which followed the river as it hugged the edges of the Moor. It twisted serenely between the islands of rocks and around the banks of silt which stretched out towards its darker depths. As we made along the riverbank, I let Max roam off the lead and he zig-zagged between the water's edge and the undergrowth tracing the smells and following their trails.

Beneath the surface, I watched the darting shapes of fish catch the sunlight before retreating to shadowed safety under the eaves of the banks. The murmuring of the water, the chatter of birds and the low hum of flies were all that broke the silence. The pace of life had slowed. There was no rush for us to arrive at St Martin's at any given time. For the first time in weeks I began to feel content and relaxed.

In less than an hour we cut off from the river and pushed our way through the grasses and wildflowers which straddled the path. As we turned a corner, the tower of St Martin's came into view. It was square, white and the stone face was weathered to a considerable degree. Work to restore it would be beyond my capabilities but I would see what I could do within the grounds.

They were indeed neglected, much more so than I had expected. However, the pathways were mostly clear, and the walkways to graves accessible. The plots themselves, with the exception of a couple which were regularly tended, had succumbed to new growth of grasses and weeds which in some cases almost obscured the headstones from view. I strolled around considering the size of the task but reasoned that, with fine weather, two weeks of hard toil would have the graveyard tidy and presentable for the new vicar. I would start at the northern end which bordered the final reaches of the Moor and work towards the church.

At the end of the path, which led towards the northern exit, I came across a small gate. It appeared to lead beyond the perimeter wall into what I assumed would be unconsecrated ground. I leant on the gate and gazed ahead. The area was in sharp contrast to the regimented order of pathways and gravestones which lay behind me. Max was enjoying the freedom of being able to snuffle and scratch his way around the grave plots. I called him to me and reattached his lead. We would go through the gate to see what lay there. The churchyard was quiet. It was one of those days when summer seemed to hold its breath.

As we approached the gate, Max suddenly became less animated. He stopped in his tracks, his ears folded flat, and a low whine emanated from the back of his throat. As I tried to move him forward the whine turned into a low growl, as if he was sensing some imminent danger of which I was unaware. It was the guttural sound of an animal in fear. He backed away from the gate shifting between a growl and a whimper which ceased only when I led him away and sat him outside the main gate.

Here he settled and obeyed my command to wait. I stroked and calmed him, wondering if it might be the smell of death lingering across the years, filling the area with a scent of decay, which his heightened senses had detected and caused him such alarm.

When I ventured back into the churchyard the air was heavy and still. Only the darting movements of dragonflies and the hovering of bees caught my eye, and only the call of a single blackbird broke the silence. Through the gate which had caused Max such distress there were brambles, twisting in sharp spirals to the sides of the flaking, brick path which had turned moss-green through damp and the absence of sunlight.

I was wary of the shadows. They were still; the strength of the sunlight removing any transparency and hiding their secrets in the hollows and thickets. A few yards away from the wall, a thin shaft of sunlight caught the edges of white stone. I stepped across into the undergrowth and carefully pushed back some strands of bracken. It was a small gravestone, covered in moss and lichen. It had lain half-hidden behind the thick layers of grass. It was unmistakably the grave of a child.

I ran back to the church and gathered some tools. A few minutes later I was hacking at the undergrowth, stripping away the constricting layers. The stone had been well protected from the weather and inscription was clear to see.

ALICE SKERRY
Died June 8th 1890
Aged 8 Years

The importance of the date was significant. I felt a nervous fear and apprehension. I had no doubt that this could all be explained away through coincidence. Many young children died in their early life, and it was not implausible that some might pass away on the same date. But this was too close to allow me to expel the tension which was taking hold of my body. The child in St Peter's churchyard, Sam Blackwood, was to meet with God on the same date in the year 1902. Could they somehow be connected? And why was Alice lying here, in unconsecrated ground, forgotten, neglected and alone?

Despite my confusion, I reasoned that the church might harbour some evidence of the child's past. I entered St. Martin's. It was dark and smelled of dust and damp wood. The windows sat high above me sending patches of dappled light to settle into the body of the church. All the doors leading from the centre were unlocked and led into rooms which contained piles of leaflets, Bibles, old posters and church ledgers.

After half an hour I found what I was looking for. In a small room off the chancel, I managed to locate the Book of Remembrance which, judging by the fur of dust on its cover, had lain untouched for some time. I carried it out into the sunshine and walked through the gate to the grave where I sat on a small mound of turf warming my bones after the sharp chill of the church. The most recent entry was over a year old, and I flicked through the damp pages eventually arriving at the entries for June 1890.

There was nothing to match the name on the gravestone from the date in question. I scanned the book believing that perhaps a message had inadvertently been written on the wrong date. But although I read in detail the entries from several months on each side of June, there was nothing.

I was about to return the volume when the pages at the back seemed to part involuntarily and a card drifted through the still air and came to rest by my feet. It was of good quality and on the front was a rose, preserved and pressed into the paper. It still maintained its bright red hue despite being held within the darkness. Below the rose, in educated writing, was simply written, 'For Alice.' It had lain between the pages of the book for over ten years.

I opened it up. On the left was a sketch in ink. It was of a young angel. It had been drawn with some skill with deference to the style of the Pre-Raphaelite artists. It had long, dark hair, was dressed in a white robe and stared at me from the page. From its eyes, tears were falling. On the right were words, written in the same meticulous hand. They read simply:

To an Angel
I knew you not in this world
May we meet in the next. Mother x

I looked pitifully at the grave. What circumstances could possibly have led to a young child being laid to rest without knowing the comfort and love that bind mother and daughter? I held the card, feeling the rough outline of the rose, inadvertency dislodging a petal which floated and twisted in the sunlight until it came to rest at the foot of the headstone.

In a moment the light changed, and the shadows were replaced with a grey veil that muted the colours of the day. The natural warmth of the sun gave way to an unwelcome chill, and spatters of rain turned patches of the gravestone from white to grey.

I turned to go, intending to return the book from whence it came, reunite with Max, and begin our journey back to Elm House. As the brightness faded, a thin light appeared through one of the windows in the church as the darkness closed around the building. It got stronger, capturing my attention until the rest of the world was an inky blackness. It flickered and beckoned. The rain shower became a torrent, and thunder rolled in the distance.

In a panic, I pushed open the stout, wooden door and stood at the rear of the church watching huge shadows sweep across the walls and the ceiling of the building. At the far end of the aisle a single, red candle burned. I held the book with all my strength and walked slowly towards it.

The air seemed to thicken, and I felt I should turn and leave, lock the door and abandon this place forever but I could not go back. The light beckoned me onward drawing me away from the shadows into the comfort of its glow. I took one last step towards it peering into the dancing colour of the flame. Then, suddenly, the church door crashed against its frame and a wind rushed between the crevices of the old timber. It surged and travelled down the aisle scattering dust and fragments of paper across the pews. It whipped around my body pulling at my shirt and hurling dust across my face. I covered my eyes in pain trying to shield them from any further onslaught. When I managed to open them again the church was in near darkness and the candle was on the floor, wax spattered across the wood like red streaks of blood radiating from an open wound.

I turned and fled. I needed to escape, and moments later I was released into the heavy, damp air with my head spinning trying to make sense of the events of the last few minutes. I implored myself to believe that the happenings were not linked to any supernatural source and that wind travelling around and buffeting the inside of an old building, where open spaces could create tunnels for air movement, was completely comprehensible. But who had lit the candle? I had seen no one that morning, and the candle was tall. It could only have been alight for a few minutes at the most. I wanted to return. The sun had reappeared, and the grounds once again looked inviting but I was wary of the shadows appearing and disappearing across the pathways and between the trees. I picked up my work bag and headed out of the church grounds. Max lay waiting in a small patch of undergrowth, my earlier command to him to 'stay' obeyed with some diligence. Outside the grounds he was calm, his normal self. He shook the rain from his coat, turned and ran in front of me towards the river. I quickened my pace and followed him home.

That evening, I lay in the darkness, mustering my thoughts, shaping the fragments of evidence which might allow me to discover the intent behind the appearances of the girl on the Moor, and possibly avert the imminent death of Sam Blackwood.

The dates of the deaths of Alice and Sam matched, and the age of the girl on the Moor was a likely match with the age of Alice at her time of death. It seemed too great a coincidence for it not to be her but these things told me nothing as to why I should be the focus of her appearances. It would seem that the girl wished to make contact. Had I been drawn to the grave deliberately to experience closer contact with her? Was it her purpose to reveal her resting place and disclose her identity to me?

The pieces were difficult to fit. I had scant additional evidence save the reaction of the woman at the caravan. Why was her reaction so hostile? Did the peg doll she clutched so tightly belong to Alice? Indeed, was she Alice's mother? It was possible, yet the writing on the card was written with some skill and suggested an educated hand. The angel too was expertly drawn, produced by someone with an artist's eye. Of course, there might be no solution. I could easily be the victim of a malevolent spirit manipulating me for its own ends, content on finding amusement with the shredding of my sanity before moving on to the next unfortunate soul.

The next day I returned with a fresh mind. The church was not far from Dunsbury Village, and I decided to make some enquiries regarding Alice and her grave. My starting point would be the public houses that were strung out along the main street or lodged in the alleys and passageways behind the village centre.

The busiest hostelry was undoubtedly the Old Ship, which stood on the bend of the main road opposite the Theologian College. It seemed to be the place that would attract passing trade and, as I stooped through its small front entrance, the bar was full of noise, banter and smoke.

'Excuse me.' I caught the eye of the barman who had just returned from changing a barrel in the cellar.

'What can I do for you, sir?' He wiped his hands on a cloth, took a tankard from the rack above the bar and motioned towards the hand pumps. 'I can recommend Dunsbury Gold. A good, refreshing ale for a summer's afternoon.'

Seeing no need to query his judgement, I let him draw the ale from the wooden pump, marvelling as he managed not to spill a single drop during the process.

'That'll be twopence.'

'May I ask you something? Do you know of a family called Skerry? They might have lived in the area some eight to ten years ago.'

He put his hand beneath his chin and thought carefully.

'Means little to me. Get so many folks passing through here but try those two over by the window. They've lived and worked in these parts for years.'

I made my way across to the far side of the room where two men, one dressed in a worn, twill jacket and the other in a black, gabardine coat sat quietly drinking. I introduced myself and explained my quest. Did they have any details of a family named Skerry who might have frequented the area?

The two men exchanged glances as if each was seeking approval from the other to respond to my question. The man in the gabardine coat looked nervous as if he was clinging to some knowledge too precious to be squandered in response to my casual inquiry. He lit a cigarette, turned away, and stared out of the window.

'Aye, we've heard of such,' uttered the man in the twill jacket. His response was sharp and unwelcoming. It bore the tone of a warning. 'It's a travellers' name. Romany if you like. They move through these parts. Camp down by the river, helping with the circus, flitting between horse fairs. Come into the village selling stuff. Cursing you if you don't buy.'

'Did you meet any of them?'

'Plenty,' muttered the man in gabardine. He turned back from the window. 'Why do you want to know?'

'I've been helping clear the grounds at St Martin's. I've discovered the grave of a young child in the unconsecrated ground, just outside the gate, on the edges of the Moor. I wondered if anyone knew what might have happened to her. The grave bears the name Alice Skerry.'

The man in the gabardine coat took a long draw on his cigarette. 'What business is it of yours?'

He sounded suspicious as if he saw some connection between the child's death and my own desire to seek out information.

'I was just curious, that's all.'

The man in the twill jacket pulled a pipe from his jacket, struck a match and sucked the flame onto the tobacco.

'There are rumours, but from years ago.'

'What rumours might I ask?'

'There was talk of child who died, shall we say in unfavourable circumstances.'

The man in the gabardine coat spoke sharply. 'Enough, Michael. We don't know him.'

'A travellers' child?'

'Perhaps.' He sipped his beer slowly and placed his glass back on the table, wiping the froth from his lips. 'Perhaps not.'

'I don't understand.'

The man in the gabardine coat became agitated, the glass in his hand shaking noticeably.

'If it's a travellers' child, it's no business of yours. Get involved in their world, and you'll most likely be cursed for the rest of your days. Make what you can of your discovery, but leave us be. We have homes, jobs and families to see to. Sharing rumours with a stranger is not a path we should be treading. Now, sir, if that's all, you may leave us in peace.'

Chapter 13
The Grave and the Doll

Despite the reaction of Max, his behaviour had brought me a degree of comfort in that he could detect unearthly signs far beyond the parameters of human senses. There would be no more surprises. He would alert me before my senses connected with any spiritual appearance, providing evidence that I was not misguided or indeed suffering from a neurosis. He would stay by my side and be my guardian. We would solve the mystery together.

I was convinced now that it was the spirit of Alice who was appearing to me. The evidence seemed to support my theory. There was the reaction of the Gypsy family by the river to my enquiries about a child and the fact that the grave bore a Romany name. In addition, Alice's age at death would be similar to that of the girl from the shadows. And then there were the rumours alluded to by the men in the Old Ship that a travellers' child had passed away in what they termed 'unfavourable circumstances'.

If my suppositions, and the theory of Andrew Donne, had any substance, I needed to find evidence of her existence to ascertain what circumstances had led to her being trapped between this world and the next. I also needed to establish her connection to myself and Sam Blackwood. Perhaps making my peace with her might prove the beginning of salvation for us both.

I decided that informing others about the grave would be a mistake. It would lead to enquiries and possibly an exhumation of the body that might serve only to exacerbate the feelings which drove the spirit to seek some kind of union with my world. Andrew's use of the word 'victim' still plagued my thinking. Although I had encountered no malevolence, I was anxious to identify why she had appeared to me. It was to my frustration that I had no understanding of her motivation and I craved some clue, some shred of evidence which might bring clarity as to why she had chosen to connect with my life.

That she was not at rest was confirmed by Max's reaction on each of our subsequent visits to St Martin's. Each day I had to leave him at the gate, return periodically to feed him, and give him comfort that I was safe and unharmed. On occasions, I tried to coax him into the churchyard, but his reaction was always the same; the low whine, the ghastly look of fear in his eyes, and the growling of a creature who had sensed a disagreeable presence within the empty paths and shadows of the graves.

Over the following few days, I tidied the grave, removing the trails of bracken and weeds that had overrun the area around the headstone. I brought cleaning materials from home and scrubbed the headstone with such determination that every last scrap of moss or lichen was washed from the surface. I then planted speedwell around the grave, small intense flowers of blue, symbolic of Christ's Resurrection, and strong enough to spread and keep the weeds at bay. And I talked.

I sat next to the grave each day, eating my lunch, telling Alice about my life and my family. I talked about the countryside and the animals, about the clouds and the blue sky, about the games I played as a child and those I would play once my own children were growing. I recounted stories from memory and details of my holidays when I was young. The process was therapeutic, and I began to feel stronger. But I felt I needed to do more.

There was a shop in one of the alleyways in Dunsbury that sold bric-a-brac salvaged from church fairs, travelling tinkers and houses of those who had left this earth. I had passed it once or twice and was sure that I might be able to find a toy; something to leave at the grave as a gift. A sign to Alice that she was in my thoughts even when I was absent from her resting place.

Outside I hesitated. The windows were dirty with broken cobwebs hanging across each pane. I could barely make out the contents that lay within, not solely because of the absence of light but because the stock had been piled together with little attempt to catalogue it into any order. For a few moments, I doubted my own sanity before I tied Max to a post and carefully pushed my way through the door. The smell of damp crept into my nostrils. The place was musty and unclean, and dust glistened in the strands of light that crept through the windows and the cracks in the brickwork.

It was crammed with all manner of paraphernalia collected or gifted to the owner over what seemed a long period of time. There were countless glass bottles, stuffed animals, skulls, and a telescope in polished brass that might have belonged to some explorer of the high seas. There was a ragged monkey holding a drum which when wound would most likely beat a discordant rhythm most disagreeable to the ears. There were swords with jewelled handles, flintlock pistols and ornate birdcages; some with their occupants filling the room with a melancholy chirruping.

The owner sat behind a counter half-obscured by two large, glass cases containing jewellery, watches and trinkets. He seemed to be dozing but with the closing of the door his eyes opened, and he nodded in greeting.

'Have you any toys which might be suitable for a young child?'

'How young?'

'About eight years old.'

'Look in there. You'll find something.'

He indicated in the direction of an old traveller's chest that was so worn it must have navigated the seven seas as the salt had weakened the leather straps and the wood was dry and cracked.

I pushed open the lid. One of the hinges gave way, and it fell in a slanted movement against a bookcase displacing some of its contents.

'Steady! Any damages must be paid for.'

The chest seemed to be filled with an assortment of toys and dolls. There were whips, balls, lead soldiers, the remains of a tea set and a clockwork train. I pulled them apart seeking to delve to the bottom of the chest but suddenly recoiled in alarm as I gazed at what lay at its wooden base. It was a doll. A child's peg doll. I was almost certain it was the one held by the traveller's wife as the caravan trundled past me on Vale Road. I pulled it from the chest. It was dirtier now. The white dress was torn and stained, but the cap with the red ribbon was there and although the stem of the rose had lost many of its leaves the flower itself was unmoved from the white lace.

'Where did you get this?' There was wavering anger in my voice which caused a look of disturbance in the owner's eyes. He leapt defensively from his seat and pointed a finger at me.

'I don't steal no things, sir. All in here is gifted or paid for.'

'I didn't suggest that. Where did you come across it?'

He shrugged and called through into the back of the shop, 'Lily, come here a minute.'

A gaunt-looking woman in a shawl parted the hanging curtain behind him and stepped into the shop.

'What?'

118

'You remember where this doll come from?'

'Who wants to know?'

'This chap here.'

'Does he want to buy it?'

I nodded.

'A shillin' and I'll tell you where it come from.'

I rummaged through my jacket pockets and handed over a silver shilling. She bit it between her yellowed teeth and dropped it into her apron pocket.'

'Ta! Right, I'll tell yer. It was brought in here by a little 'un about three months ago. Just waltzed in brazen as yer like and plonked it on the counter. Said she didn't want it no more and didn't want anything for it neither.' She paused looking me up and down. 'She did say, though, that someone would come to claim it. That's why we shoved it at the bottom of the trunk. She said it would be a young man, well-dressed and clean-shaven.'

'What did she look like?'

'Easy! Never forget her. She was about eight years old, scrawny as a rake handle and looked like death. Oh, yes and she had thick black hair, but I couldn't see most of it because of her cloak.'

* * * * * *

There was no wind, just the still warmth of a midsummer's afternoon. A haze settled across the graveyard. Insects and bob seeds seemed to be held in the sun's rays which arrowed through the trees and flickered on the pathways, verges and headstones. In the weeks I had tended the grounds I had met hardly any visitors. The church was small, and the Sunday congregation consisted of only a handful of attendees, most of whom seemed to be in their later years. I

119

felt that the grounds were mine to roam and enjoy in splendid isolation from the pressure and worries that ordinary living can bring.

I had stripped the majority of tangled foliage from around the graves, and the pathways were fresh and clean. I had pinned back the gate leading into the unconsecrated ground. I wanted any spirits who resided beyond the church to feel that there was an open pathway to redemption should they choose to tread it.

I pulled the peg doll from my work bag and sat at the side of Alice's grave. I explained to her that I had collected it as she had wished and returning it was my gift. I hoped that she treated this act as a mark of friendship between us and that she would take me as a friend of her own. I secured it sitting between two small plant pots that contained white daisies, said a silent prayer and left for home.

That night a storm came. Sheets of rain, illuminated by bursts of lightning, drove across the sky and explosions of thunder rocked the very fabric of Elm House. I lay in bed, fully awake, watching the harsh shadows appear and disappear with each flash of raw energy. I feared for the state of the graveyard, the newly embedded plants and the smooth, swept pathways. I worried about Alice's doll which would now surely be drenched to the point of destruction. I prayed Alice had connected with its spirit and that my good intentions were not being washed away in the forceful deluge.

The next morning I rose early and made my way to the churchyard. The rain clouds had dissipated, but the Mersey was swollen to the point where its banks strained to hold back the torrents that tested the strength of every curve and inlet. From the river I trod a path of mud and by the time I reached the church I had to pause to remove the excess layers that clogged my boots and spattered the bottom of my trousers. The pathways inside the grounds were clear. The water had run away in rivers creating smooth, soiled surfaces much like a beach after a newly receded tide.

I was first to tread the path to Alice's grave, and I approached in trepidation. It was, however, much as I had left if the previous afternoon, save for the damage the weight of rain had wrought on its immediate surroundings. The grass around the grave glistened as the sunlight flickered across its sodden surface. The daises lay flat, engulfed by pools of water which drained over the side of the pots. From between them, I took the doll. It was bone dry. Its hair and surfaces protected by a piece of moleskin which had been laid around it like a dark cloak.

.

Chapter 14
Celebration

The following morning I took the train from Cedar Moor Station into Manchester and made my way towards the university. If Andrew had attained his ambition of continuing his studies in Manchester, then enquiries at the university might lead me to his whereabouts.

I strolled quickly down Oxford Road and in a few minutes I stood outside the entrance to the University. I marvelled at the imposing nature of the great stone arcade with its granite piers, which led through to the quadrangle, sheltered by a rhythm of buttresses and dominant towers which threw long shadows across the lawns and pathways. The building had been completed less than thirty years ago, but it seemed as if had stood on this plot of land for centuries, its modern Gothic architecture evoking thoughts of grotesque tales that might lay undiscovered inside the walls of such a haunting building.

I decided that my first port of call would be the administration office, but as I made my way through the iron gates a large, white poster caught my eye.

Faculty of Religion and Theology
Early Enlightenment in the 18th and 19th Centuries
A Scottish Perspective
A Talk by A G Donne, Edinburgh University
Today in the Main Library 10am – 12pm

The time was just after midday, and I hurried up the flight of stone steps which led to the university's main library. There I found Andrew chatting with a colleague and scribbling furiously into his leather notebook. I stood close by letting him complete his task before catching his eye and moving forwards.

He rose animatedly, almost tipping over his heavy wooden chair, and thrust his hand welcomingly into mine.

'Adam. Wonderful to see you. Sincere apologies that I have not written to you. I had the good fortune to be offered a post-graduate place here at the university. My plans to join the Theologian College were thrown into disarray. But no matter. I know why you are here. There can be but one reason. We must find a place where we can talk in private. Follow me.'

We hastened through the college grounds, passing students and professors, all hurrying about their business and each one seemingly burdened with armfuls of books and rolled manuscripts. The Salutation public house was a charming hostelry with a cluster of small rooms, and we settled comfortably into an unoccupied corner, a glass of strong ale in each of our hands.

'How do you like Manchester?'

Andrew smiled and looked out of the window across to the spires of the university building and beyond.

'It is a great city of the age, Adam. It has so much to offer that will enrich my studies. I have been lucky to leave one centre of academic excellence for another. I have outstanding tutors and have learned much in a very short time. But you have not come to converse about me. The girl. She has visited you again?'

I outlined the series of events since our last meeting: my illness, the discovery of the grave, the mysteries of the doll and the candle, the concurrence of the dates of death on each headstone. I told him of my furtive attempts to find anything or anyone in my past which might offer a connection with either the girl or Sam Blackwood. Andrew listened, jotting down the odd note as I spoke. He drank a good half of his beer, slowly savouring the taste, wiped his mouth with the back of his hand, and sat back.

'Let us try to be objective about all this. The grave in the churchyard which appeared and disappeared was that of Sam Blackwood?'

'Yes, I'm certain.'

'And it contained a date in the future when he meets his death?'

'Yes. The 8th of June next year, so at this moment he must be alive, walking this earth unaware of his impending fate.'

'Unless, of course, it is a child yet to be born. Which might explain why you can find no trace.'

'Then he would have to be less than a year old when he dies.'

'He would. You have to understand, Adam that we are working with forces outside the comprehension of our minds. If this girl, this spirit, has travelled from the future then she will know all that we do not. We cannot battle with that. We must accept what is occurring, and if possible try to shift events so that the girl, the spirit, no longer feels it necessary to connect with your world.'

'But how can I do that?'

'Are you sure this manifestation that comes to you is a girl?'

'Yes. I was unsure at first, but with every appearance her form becomes more substantial. When she appeared after the wedding, she was there. A girl. A child in a black cloak.'

'So about the same age as Alice Skerry, who died in 1890, also on the 8th of June.

'Yes. I am certain it is her. The occurrences in the churchyard and around her grave would seem to confirm so.'

'Then we must explore these points of connection.'

He leaned across the table and took hold of my arm. 'If Alice is the link, Adam, there must be something which binds you in some way. The candle could be a plea for help, a desire for light to ease her from the darkness. She may see you as the pathway. There is a triangle here, Adam, between yourself, Alice, if she is the spirit, and Sam Blackwood. Do you have any clues to Alice's life?'

'The only thing was the card. It was in the book of remembrance at St Martin's Church. It was from her mother who she never knew.'

'Then she is your key, Adam. Find her and the connection will be made.'

* * * * * *

I had completed all that was required of me at St Martin's. The gardens were revived and on summer days looked resplendent surrounded by wandering pathways and tidy grave plots. I had arranged for a sum of money to be provided to accommodate half a dozen benches thoughtfully placed to catch the threads of sunlight that slanted through the canopy of trees. The church congregation had shown a significant increase, and I had received thanks from the vicar who commended me for what he termed 'most charitable work.'

My greatest reward was to come shortly after I arrived home on the last Friday in July. I was met by Clara who grabbed my hand and swept me into our living room where she insisted I sit to hear her news. That afternoon she had been to see Dr Jacobs who had confirmed that she was two months pregnant. Our child would be born in March, and we would become the family that we had always wished for.

She had told no one else but would announce the news to the family that evening.

We were both uplifted. I was beginning to feel much stronger and my sleep had returned to a normal pattern. I felt that I had made my peace with Alice and that Andrew would be proud of my efforts. I no longer feared to gaze into shadows or venture alone through empty parks or remote areas of the Moor. It had been a full two months since our honeymoon in Edinburgh, and there had been no further sightings of the girl.

That night we celebrated. The family members gathered at Elm House and there was talk of the future and happiness and new life. In the coming years, there would be much to look forward to and the impending marriage of Grace to David would complete the family circle.

Joseph was a happy man, but the level of contentment in Mary's eyes did not shine brightly. I noticed the same reticence of spirit as on the night of our own engagement celebrations. A muted smile was fixed on her face, and her coldness of spirit was at odds with the warm celebrations that filled the room. For the majority of the evening, she sat in hushed conversation with Hattie. I assumed the occasional tears trickling from her eyes were ones of happiness, but when the clock struck ten she rose quietly, bade us all good night, and retired to bed.

* * * * * *

Over the next few days I thought in some depth about Andrew's advice. However, I considered I had reached a watershed and that there was little more I could do. In my free time I had explored the parish records and searched the dusty shelves and cupboards of St Martin's but if there were any clues to the identity of Alice's mother they seemed to have been lost or never recorded. There were no records of Alice's birth and death in the local registers and the only clue I had was the card with the rose and the angel. If she was from a travelling family and her real mother had moved on after her death, there was little hope of finding any connection some eight years later.

I could hypothesise about the life of Alice. She had at some point been tragically parted from her real mother, for whatever reason I could not imagine. No doubt there were circumstances within the travelling community where this might happen. There could have been any number of reasons for her death and the location of her resting place was compassionately made known to her real mother to allow her to pay her final respects.

Sam Blackwood was different though. I had no such ideas as to his connection with Alice. She had drawn my attention to his grave, but the reason was unknown to me. Andrew had posed the idea that the child was yet to be born. Clara and I were about to start our own family? Were Alice's appearances a means of alerting us to a family tragedy? If so, she had already succeeded. If Clara gave birth to a son we would not bless him with the name, Sam.

I wanted to believe that this was the solution. That Alice's appearances to me were a gift and that she was a compassionate child who wished those more fortunate than herself should live happy and fulfilling lives. I hoped that perhaps her mission was complete. She had delivered the warning and trusted me to play a part in her salvation. In my conversations at her graveside I had told her that when my strength was recovered, and those who knew me were assured of my own well-being, I would approach the church and explore all avenues which might lead to her being reinterred in consecrated ground. I felt a quiet certainty that I had made my peace with her and that she understood that I would help her find her own.

Chapter 15
A Child Is Born

The Christmas of 1901 was one of the happiest times of my life. Indeed my health was such that a fortnight before the festivities, I completed my outstanding jobs for the church, attended the bank for a meeting with Mr Tomkins, and a manager from Head Office, and was told that all things being well I could return to my position on the 6th of January.

There had been no more appearances of Alice, and I had regularly tended her grave, providing fresh flowers and further stories of my plans for the future and how I should set in motion the business of moving her into consecrated ground.

Over the last few months, however, one absent thought had crept back into my thinking. It lodged in my mind, and I required a satisfactory explanation. On the day of our wedding, as I was engulfed in the confusion of having seen the girl and the gravestone, I was sure that the woman I had seen flitting across the outskirts of the churchyard was Edith Murdstone. Was it possible that she had craved an invite to the ceremony but was no longer on good terms with Joseph? Had she remained on the periphery of the wedding shielding her presence from those who might recognise her?

If it was her, she was almost within touching distance of the girl and must surely have seen her. If Alice had lived in Cedar Moor for even a small part of her eight years, she might have recognised her and have some clue to her fate.

I had purposefully kept away from Laurel House. In my fragile mental state I was wary of pursuing further lines of investigation that might conflict with my decision to suppress the events of the past few months from my thoughts. I wanted to concentrate only on the positives that future happiness would bring.

I had not encountered Mrs Murdstone since leaving for Elm House the week after our wedding. I found it a little strange that, given the size of Cedar Moor and its sparsity of population, I should not have seen her around the shops or taking a leisurely stroll in the park directly opposite the gates of her home. Nevertheless, that afternoon I made my way over to her house. I knocked only once on the door, and she attended immediately, smiling and beckoning me through into the morning room.

'Mr Blackwood, this is a pleasant surprise. I assume your young wife has not expelled you from the house and you are looking for lodgings?'

'No.' I smiled, 'Nothing like that. We are the happiest couple you could wish to meet. Did you manage to see us on the day of the wedding?'

'What brings you here, Mr Blackwood?' There was a discernible change in her tone as if I had said something inappropriate.

'Mrs Murdstone, as I came out of the church after the ceremony, I thought I saw a young girl in the grounds kneeling by a gravestone.' I took a breath. 'I thought I caught a glimpse of you nearby and I was wondering, if it was you, did you recognise the girl?'

'This is the same girl you told me about when you first lodged here? The girl whom I suggested to you would most probably be a street urchin?'

'That's right. I have no reason to doubt your wisdom, but I would just like to know who she is.'

She rose from her chair, put down her cup, and moved over to sit next to me on the settee.

'Adam, Cedar Moor is a small place. I know of your circumstances and your illness of the last few months. There may be a girl, but she will be of this earth. She will be, as I suggested before, a child of the streets, a travellers' daughter. You must leave this all behind and proceed with your life. I was not there on the day. I was given a personal invitation from Joseph, but I could not attend. My sister had fallen sick. On the day of your wedding, I was in Shrewsbury, some sixty miles from here.'

* * * * * *

It was to everyone's joy that Clara gave birth to a baby girl on March 14th. There were no complications and within an hour of the birth I was in her room at Elm House holding my daughter and overwhelmed with happiness.

It was Hattie's reaction, however, that was the cause of some puzzlement. She arrived at the house shortly before the birth and was more animated than I had ever seen her. It seemed not just a state of excitement and anticipation but one of extreme anxiety. She could not remain still for more than a few moments, sitting and rising and continually looking for something to occupy each second until the birth was announced. When the doctor finally emerged from the room and announced the birth of a girl Hattie fell silent, sitting swiftly upon a chair, tears streaming from her eyes. My first thoughts were that they were tears of happiness, but on observing her closely, I could see that she was shaking. Howard seemed unconcerned by her distress, and I felt the need to in some way try to comfort her.

'Would you like a brandy?' It seemed an inappropriate thing to say, but our relationship had always been distant, and I could think of no personal approach which might settle her unease. To my surprise, she nodded, and I poured her a decent measure which she accepted gratefully.

She sat gazing out of the window, the effect of the alcohol having some measure of success in calming her shaking which was now barely noticeable.

'Are you all right? Can I do anything? Would you like me to ask Howard to take you home?'

She shook her head. 'No, I was momentarily overcome by joy for you and Clara, it made me think back to....' She paused and coughed as if deliberately suppressing the words that would have finished the sentence. She steadied herself. 'It took me back to a happier time.' A fresh tear fell slowly onto her hand, and she wiped it away swiftly with her handkerchief. 'I am full of happiness for you and Clara,' she paused again, 'but I so wish she had given birth to a boy.'

I took this rather a strange comment but concluded that being an aunt to the articulate and tireless Thomas, she was somewhat swayed to underestimate the joys that a baby girl could bring into a family. Clara and I were delighted, and the fact that both she and the child were well was a more important consideration than that of its sex.

* * * * * *

Eventually, we came to the naming of the girl. Clara and her sisters were engrossed in family research, seeing if a name from grandparents or even more distant relatives might suggest something more individual than those in current favour such as Helen, Anna, Ruth or Elizabeth. Rosie was the most enthusiastic of the girls. She had a fine knowledge of family history and was enthralled by many of the beautiful names that came from both sides of the family. She discovered that the girls' great, great grandmother had been named Jessamine and was a strong woman of brash opinions and thoughts who could hold sway on any subject on an equal footing with the men of the family. She had lived into her nineties and raised four fine boys.

The suggestion met with general approval. Clara was a lover of nature and had considered some names with floral connections that were currently in vogue such as Primrose, Daisy and Beryl. We liked the classical spelling, rather than the more modern, Jasmine, although for my part I felt the old name was a little too long and slightly cumbersome. After many hours of discussion, Clara and I agreed that it would be the child's second name and that her Christian name would be Lucy which was gaining a foothold in popularity from the French. We felt that the meaning of the name, connected as it was with dawn and the rising of light, would suit a child born on the threshold of summer days.

After all was settled, I felt that I had to say something to Clara to see if she could offer me some insight into the difference in personality between Rosie and Hattie. That Hattie's behaviour was an outward sign of discontent or misery was without question. It had been something that had puzzled me since I had first met her, but it seemed to be accepted, or ignored, by the other members of the family. I wondered if Hattie knew about Rosie's adoption and that perhaps she held a brooding resentment that her position as firstborn into the family had been usurped. Rosie was the spark, the perfectionist and rule-keeper. She was the one to whom Grace and Clara looked for guidance; a new woman of intelligence and organisation.

Lucy was asleep, and we sat in the drawing-room in front of the fire which threw out its last offerings of warmth as we approached the time to retire to bed. I chose the moment to delve casually into family history.

'It must have been very fulfilling to share your childhood with sisters who are so different in their ways.'

Clara looked at me quizzically. 'Everyone is different, Adam. What exactly do you mean?'

'Well, you and Grace are quite similar. Two bright stars born out of the confidence of having the knowledge and support of older siblings. Rosie, of course, is the one you all look up to. She is confident, articulate with the ability to converse with anyone on the issues of the day. She is quite matriarchal but treats you all as her equals.' I paused, trying to secure the right words to describe Hattie without seeming to be concerned or over critical. 'Hattie seems to be quite aloof at times. She seems to prefer quiet moments rather than engagement in any animated discourse.'

I could have put things a little better, but Clara seemed to understand what I was saying. She rose from her chair and sat close to me.

'I do have something to tell you, Adam. You are my husband who I love and trust, but you must promise you will never breathe a word of what I am about to say to anyone. Some years ago we made a promise to mother that what I am about to tell you should never be spoken of within our family circle.'

Her voice dropped almost to a whisper and tears fell softly from her eyes.

'Hattie was not always like she is now. She was full of life, the centre of attention, a free spirit. Everyone delighted in her presence. Her marriage to Howard should have been the beginning of a wonderful life for them both. All things were perfect, and Hattie gave birth to a child in the spring of 1894. She was a sweet baby girl named Ellen-Marie, in whom we all delighted but....' she paused trying to compose herself as more tears fell and her hands started to shake,

'....the poor child died suddenly. She was only a few months old.'

'Good grief. How did this happen?'

'As it happens to so many children, Adam. It was a cold spring which lingered into early summer. The air seemed permanently damp. She caught a chill which developed into pneumonia and she passed away quickly.'

'How devastating for them both. What a misfortune for them to bear. And they have never tried for another child?'

'Hattie was heartbroken, Adam. She shut out the world for months. Mother decided the child should never be spoken of again. It was her way of helping Hattie move on. You must promise me you will speak of this to no one.'

'Of course. Does the child rest in St Peter's graveyard?'

Clara leant across and clasped my hand.

'Adam, I have a confession to make and I pray that you will be understanding.'

Her hand tightened on mine and I could see the tension gather in her face.

'She is not in St Peter's Churchyard, Adam. She is far away from here. They were staying in Edinburgh at the time of her death. She rests in Greyfriars Kirk. It was my reason for taking you there. I wanted so much to see her grave. I wanted to lay some flowers and say a prayer. I tried to force myself to tell you but the conflict between remaining silent and allowing you to know the truth was too much for me. I had to turn and walk away. Adam, please believe me when I say I wanted to tell you and confide in you but mother had made me promise never to speak of it.'

Clara's hand was now tightly clasped around my own and she was shaking. I held her close and reassured her that I understood and that I was grateful that she had found the strength to confide in me despite the promise to her mother.

I took her handkerchief and wiped away some tears that had fallen in soft streaks across her face.

'Do you know why she was laid to rest in Edinburgh?'

'I was only sixteen at the time, Adam. I was told only of her death and resting place. It was not my place to ask questions.'

She rose and made her way from the room to see to Lucy and I was left alone with my thoughts.

I sat for a few minutes gazing into the embers of the fire. It seemed that my arrival in Cedar Moor had swept me into a world where my mind was constantly wrangling with questions beyond my capability to answer. What other secrets lay sheltered and cloaked within the family waiting for me to stumble across as the years progressed? I was already carrying the weight of Rosie's parentage. If more were hidden I had no doubt they would rise. Things buried away have a habit of clawing themselves to the surface over time and one day bursting open like an ugly wound.

I felt like an outsider, someone to be kept at arm's length, uninvited into the intimate history of the family. But the warmth and happiness of summer beckoned, and I was determined it would be one in which I would concentrate on our family and enjoy the first golden months of Lucy's life.

Chapter 16
Glamis.

Within a fortnight of the birth, Clara and I were called into Joseph's study where he sat behind his desk, a sea of paperwork spread out in front of him.

'I've decided it's time for me to think about spreading my assets. I'm not a young man, and I would like to see the benefit of them enjoyed by my family before I die. With this in mind, I have been thinking about your future and the need for you to have your own place. Elm House is fine for your immediate needs but as your family grows you will need independence and a place to call your own. I've spoken with my solicitor and arranged to purchase a suitable property for you both. I have a client from Scotland who is looking to sell a property quickly and he owes me a debt of thanks for my assistance with some profitable purchases of farmland in the Highlands. The house is a single detached residence. It will be ideal for a growing family and is just a short walk from here. A family has been renting the property for the past year but will shortly be moving south. This weekend they are visiting friends in Liverpool, and it will be an appropriate time for you to view the house and establish whether it feels like a place in which you could settle.

Clara rushed forward and embraced her father with some force. It was obvious that he was unaccustomed to such affection as he visibly reddened and hesitated to close his arms around her.

On Saturday morning we left Lucy with Mary and strolled with Max and Joseph to Park Grove, a small lane that crept towards the edges of the Moor. The house sat alone at the far end of the lane. It had a pleasant view, and the oak trees on each side of the path provided a welcoming canopy of shade and light, framing the entrance to the house as if it were a painting of an idyllic country retreat. On the white, barred gate was a new wooden plaque bearing its name, 'Glamis'.

It was being rented by a young family who had no shortage of money. The husband traded on the Manchester Stock Market and had been promoted by his company to a job in London. Joseph explained that they were leaving with regret as they loved the area with its mix of shops, open spaces and fresh air.

The family were already packing their possessions, and the rooms seemed large and empty. Nonetheless, Clara was filled with excitement and wandered through the house with an eye to furnishings and decoration. While she busied herself with note-taking, I wandered into the grounds. The area close to the house had been cleared and contained a garden bench, some small ornaments and a children's swing.

The garden seemed to drift away becoming indistinguishable at its furthest point from the tangled undergrowth of the Moor. I could just identify the remains of a rotting fence, its panels cracked and strangled by aggressive roots which turned and twisted from the ground as if ready to snare any unsuspecting person who might roam casually amongst them. Beyond, I could make out the dark shape of the rising land, rolling on for miles towards the Pennine Hills. Max was drawn to the smells of damp and decay and I noticed the pungent smell of lilies and the distinctive aroma of wild garlic which had been encouraged to grow around the rear entrance to the house. The air felt damp and I became aware of the rise and fall of the wind. The pattering of rain on trees forced me to return indoors.

'Do we know the history of the property?' Clara was taken to proceed with the purchase, but I felt I needed to ask Joseph what he knew about its recent past.

'The important thing is that the man is letting me have it at a reasonable price. Its history is a secondary consideration but I do know he bought it two years ago, lived here for a short time and then decided he would move back to Scotland. True, it needs some work to get it back into shape but once completed it will be a fine property.'

'Do you know why it is called 'Glamis'?'

'No idea,' muttered Joseph. 'He named the place. I assume it has some meaningful association with his past.' With that he moved on and turned the talk to other matters.

* * * * * *

It had been four weeks since we signed the preliminary papers and in just two weeks the moving day would arrive.

It was a warm Saturday in April when we took a visit to Glamis where, Mr and Mrs Bryant had consented to us undertaking some preliminary measurements for carpets, curtains and other household fixtures.

'We hope you will be as happy here as we have been.' Henry Bryant shook my hand vigorously, and his wife smiled warmly as if there was comfort in the knowledge that the house was being placed into good hands with the prospect of children like their own running and hiding in its rooms, attic, cellars and the twisted undergrowth of the garden.

'Thank you!'

It was understandable that their children, Jack and Annie, were excited at the prospect of the journey to London. They were animated, talkative and eager to share their elation with us both. I shook Jack's hand to wish him good luck and farewell.

'Well, Jack, what will you miss most about the house?'

'Everything!' he shouted, and then turned to look at his sister and shook his head. 'Well, not quite everything.'

'Not quite everything?'

'It's her! He pointed accusingly at Annie.

'Oh, not again,' bemoaned Mrs Bryant. 'Jack, will you get that silly idea out of your head.'

Annie glowered at her brother.

Mrs Bryant shooed them away and invited us both into the parlour where her maid brought us afternoon refreshments of tea and lemon cake. We chatted pleasantly about the house and our plans for the future. After an hour or so we felt we knew them well and there was a fleeting sorrow that they would not be staying in the area.

As we left to return home, Annie hurtled down the stairs and skidded to a halt on the polished, oak floor. 'Mother, will you please tell Jack to stop the lies he is telling about me. I never leave my room at night. I should be too scared to do so.'

Mrs Bryant ruffled Annie's hair and whispered, 'Later.' She turned to us apologetically. 'I'm so sorry, children can be so bothersome, but this has been going on for some time now.'

'Nothing serious, I hope.'

Mrs Bryant smiled at us both. 'Childish imagination running wild, I'm afraid. Jack imagines Annie is creeping into his room after lights out. He says she enters and disappears as if she were a fleeting shadow.'

'What kind of shadow?'

'Mrs Bryant smiled. 'Well, I would imagine one which pertains to the shape of a young girl like his sister.'

Annie clung to her mother's skirt, peering innocently at Clara and myself. Then she turned and ran, her wisps of long, dark hair flowing around her pale features as she disappeared into the darkness of the house.

Chapter 17
Discovery.

Our move to Glamis proceeded. There was much to do. Clara busied herself with the organisation of tradesmen and decorators and within the month the vestiges of the previous occupants had all but vanished. The rooms were bright and welcoming and Joseph had arranged for a team of landscape gardeners to attend to the grounds. The sun shone, through the windows, through the trees and into the soul of our lives. There was happiness within the walls but a feeling that we were not alone.

On a clear spring evening I sat peacefully in the garden. Alice had appeared to me only twice in any substantial form, but she was here settling in my presence unable to be cast away. More worryingly, she was touching the lives of children of a similar age. My fear was not for my own safety but for that of Thomas and Jack. Were they connected in some way to Sam Blackwood? And might their own graves, with the date of their future deaths appear, to toss me into even greater depths of anxiety and confusion?

My thoughts turned to leaving Cedar Moor. I poured myself a drink and sat for some moments revisiting the time before my arrival. It was barely eighteen months since I had stepped from the train and into the world of my dark companion. The pull of leaving was strong. I would ask Mr Tomkins about the possibility of a transfer to another branch. I thought of Yorkshire, its homely towns and picturesque dales. As the effect of the alcohol soothed my anxiety, I saw our life together away from the constricting presence of the girl on the Moor.

I finished the brandy and returned to our room intent on examining my contract of employment to see if there were any terms which might prevent me from requesting such a transfer. I leafed through the contents of my briefcase but could find no trace of it, nor some other pieces of paperwork that I had brought from Bolton, including my birth certificate and my references from my previous employer.

I wracked my brains. I had certainly brought them with me, but after a thorough search they were nowhere to be found within our rooms. I concluded that the most likely place I might find them was in Edith Murdstone's filing cabinet in the cellar of her home. I had a vague recollection of asking her to let me store them in a place of safety, and I knew that was where she kept all her important papers.

The following evening I took the short stroll across the Moor to Laurel House. It was around 7.00 pm, and I was sure that Mrs Murdstone would be at home, not least providing a hearty tea for her guests who would be settling in after a hard day's work. To my surprise, there were no lights visible as I trod the gravelled drive and my loud knocks on the front door provoked no response from within.

Supposing she might be at the rear of the property enjoying the evening sunshine that was settling across the Moor, I made my way down the narrow path and through the side gate only to find the garden deserted. I was about to leave when I noticed the rear door was slightly ajar. With the realisation that perhaps the house had been burgled and Mrs Murdstone had come to some harm, a sense of worry started to rise within me.

I entered in trepidation, carefully pushing the door open and silently treading into the scullery. There were no signs of entry to the house. All was in order, and there were no footprints on the polished, stone-flagged floor.

'Mrs Murdstone!' My voice echoed through the hallway and up into the body of the landing, but there was no reply. The house was silent. After a few more shouts and exploration of the rooms on the upper and ground floors, I realised I was alone. There were no guests. Neither did it appear any had lately undertaken residence at the house. All the rooms on the upper floor were locked bar one. In Mrs Murdstone's room the bed was made and all things on the dressing table and other surfaces were in a neat order.

I reasoned that she had left to visit a friend and had absent-mindedly left the rear door unlocked. Perhaps she had been enjoying the afternoon sunshine. Perhaps the heat and warmth had lulled her senses; an easy thing to happen when even a short period in the sun can slow the mind and relax the brain to the point of forgetfulness.

I was not sure what to do. After all, I was an intruder in the house, but the cellar door was unlocked, and I decided there would be no harm in seeing if I could gain access to the filing cabinet and recover my documents. My footsteps echoed on the stone steps as I made my way down into the cool chamber but entering from the brightness of a summer's day my eyes could not seem to get used to the darkness. I made my way back to the kitchen where I lit a candle and carried it carefully in its holder back down into the depths of the house.

My shadow jumped and flickered across the walls. The cellar was clean, the floor recently swept and there in the corner was the filing cabinet with an array of papers arranged in an orderly manner on a table next to it, as if to invite me to consider their contents and purpose. I gathered them up and climbed the stairs quickly. Back in the kitchen, I spread the documents on the kitchen table. There indeed was the envelope containing my important papers and I placed them safely into my briefcase. Intent on returning Mrs Murdstone's personal items back to where they would be stored securely I quickly gathered them up. I made swiftly for the cellar but in my haste I allowed a large brown envelope to drop from the pile. It came to rest at the top of the steps as if determined to halt my progress. It was old and time-worn. On the front was written simply written 'Alice'. The envelope was sealed.

I had no choice. I knew what I was about to do was wrong but I felt compelled to open it. I took a knife from the kitchen drawer, my heart pounding should Mrs Murdstone return and find me in such an inopportune situation. I carefully slit open the envelope and removed its contents. There were several documents. The first was a birth certificate. I moved into the light and with trembling hands managed to make out the details recorded on its surface. It was a record of the birth of a child, Alice Wood, with the date recorded as April 10th, 1882. The place of birth was Manchester. The mother was recorded as Edith Wood of Cedar Moor. In the space reserved for father, there was merely written, 'Unknown'.

A mixture of feelings swept through me. In my panic, I had assumed that the birth certificate would relate to Alice Skerry and that it would lead me to some connection that would allow me to solve the mystery of her parentage and the reason why she came to lie in unconsecrated ground. That this was not the case gave rise to disappointment. The mystery would not be solved, and I would continue to spend my days hoping that the child was at rest and would no longer feel the desire to bridge into the world of the living.

However, whatever feelings I had suddenly gave way to acute feelings of apprehension and unease. Beneath the envelope which I had plucked from the table lay another. It was the same size, weathered brown with the same handwriting on the front and the same inscription, simply 'Alice'.

I picked it up with hardly the strength to ease the white parchment from the body of the envelope. For a moment, I prayed my eyes were deceiving me and that I was a victim of some trick of the imagination It was the death certificate for Alice Skerry. Her date of birth was identical to the previous document: April 10th 1882. The cause of death on 8th June 1890 was given as 'circulatory disease and pneumonia' with the place of death, Cedar Moor. I had found her at last.

I struggled to pull the pieces together. I wanted to believe that this was some wild coincidence and that they were two different children. I wanted to believe that Alice Wood was alive and well, a young woman of 20 years old who now lived apart from her mother in some town or city away from Manchester.

I clawed through the documents which lay before me. There was a letter from the same year addressed to Edith Wood. The writing on the front was clear. I knew the handwriting. It was that of Joseph Jackson. I glanced around and moved to the window, closing and bolting the back door as I gazed in disbelief at the story unfolding through the words of Joseph resurrected from over twenty years ago.

Edith,

I am glad we have been able to arrive at a mutual agreement for you to leave my employment. The events of the last few months have taken a toll on us both. We have done our best for the child. She will be cared for and grow up knowing nothing of her real parentage. I trust that my offer of financial help

*and a place to live will meet with your approval and
that we can put all this behind us and lead happy and
fulfilling lives.*

Joseph.

I stared in disbelief, letting the documents fall to the
table. Alice Wood and Alice Skerry were the same child.
What demons had I uncovered and what now should I do
being the holder of such wretched information? I gathered
the documents together, intent on returning them to the
filing cabinet. Perhaps I could convince myself that I had
never encountered them and that they could lie locked away,
undisturbed in their resting place. How could I release such
hidden secrets into a family at a point of happiness and joy?
How could I inflict such suffering on Mary and her
daughters? I held them in my hand, turning from the
window to make my descent into the cellar. My route was
blocked by Edith Murdstone who had entered through the
front door.

She gazed at the bundle of documents in my hand which
were creasing under the nervous pressure I was exerting on
them.

'I prayed this day would never come.' Her voice wavered
with emotion. Tears fell from her eyes. She stumbled past
me and sat on a kitchen chair holding her face in trembling
hands.

'You had no right!' she sobbed. 'Who put you up to this?
Do you want money? Joseph gave me plenty. You can take it
all for your cursed family.'

I sat at the table opposite her struggling to steady my
voice. The facts presented to me were capable of fatally
splitting our family apart. I needed to hear the details from a

woman who had endured the years of silent pain before I could form a plan of action which might deliver some kind of resolution.

'I was not here to pry and it was improper of me to enter your house when you were not here. Please accept I came only to recover some personal documents. It was by accident that I fell upon the certificates and the letter. I have found her grave.'

Mrs Murdstone lifted her face and stared disbelievingly at me. 'He wouldn't tell me. He said it was for the best that I should never know. That I should wipe all memory of her. He told me all had been arranged and that she would rest in peace. Where is she?'

'But surely you know. I found your card in the book of remembrance.'

'Joseph took the card. He allowed me to write it as one last parting act. He never told me where she was.'

I explained to her how I had come across the grave but withheld my thoughts on the other events that had plagued me since Alice's first appearance. It felt like an intrusion on her grief but I did need to ask her one question.

'Have you any knowledge of a Sam Blackwood?'

She looked at me quizzically. 'I have never encountered that name. Is he a relative of yours?'

I shook my head. 'I'm not sure. I came across the name in the graveyard at St Peter's and wondered if I might trace his ancestry.'

I told her nothing about him being a child of the future, nor that his date of death was but three months away on the very anniversary of her daughter's. I had to make the connection, but this was no time to delve into Edith Murdtone's past. Nor did I need to. She wiped her eyes, sat calmly at the table and related the events which had haunted her for so many years.

She was a young woman of twenty-six when she commenced work as Joseph's personal assistant at the cotton mill. There had been an instant attraction between them, and after a short time, they became lovers. After a few months, Edith became pregnant, and Joseph urged her to get rid of the child. She refused, and he paid for her to move to a house in Manchester where the child was born. Edith planned to return to Cedar Moor, but Joseph was adamant that the child must be dealt with. He arranged for her to be taken into the care of a travelling circus family who camped near to his factory. There was money involved and threats. Joseph was a powerful man who people would resist at their peril. She named the girl Alice but there was no time for a baptism, and the child was handed to the family who immediately left the area.

I listened intently as she delivered the facts unemotionally, speaking as if she had put some distance between herself and the reality of the situation. There had been promises from Joseph, unfulfilled. She was young and naive and believed they might have a future together but, of course, it all came to nothing, and she agreed to remain silent and accept his favours. He gave her substantial amounts of money and allowed her to return to Shaw House to live. She paused to steady her thoughts, and I brought her a glass of water which she accepted thankfully.

'I don't understand. If Alice was taken away, how does she lie at St Martin's Church?'

'They returned, one stormy night in June 1890. Alice was ill. She had been coughing and vomiting for some hours. The couple called at Joseph's house begging for money to call a doctor. He dragged them down the path and threatened to set the dogs on them. The next day they returned to tell him Alice had died. They threatened him with the police, and he paid them off which a substantial sum of money. He told me he had arranged with a local undertaker to take the body and she would be laid to rest.'

More tears fell from her eyes. 'Years later Joseph let me know that she was asking for me, her mother. They must have revealed her parentage before she died.'

'I saw you running across the graveyard at my wedding.' I hesitated, looking into her eyes which gazed blankly into mine. 'She comes to you too. You knew she would appear on my wedding day. You knew when I brought you the sketch of the girl I had seen in the park. What does she want of me? Am I in some sort of danger? Tell me.'

Mrs Murdstone shook her head. 'I only witness the appearance of the grave sometimes. I used to think it was my imagination caused by mourning and a mother's overwhelming guilt. Alice's name appears on the gravestone.' Her voice fell, and she spoke in a monotone. 'But it can change. It depends on whoever is next.'

'What do you mean by next?'

'She is not at rest, Adam. She cannot forgive. She does it to haunt me, to torture me as I can only watch events, knowing that there may be no end, until...'

'Until when?'

'Until we are all forgiven, Adam...or all punished.'

'I'm not sure I understand. You are saying she seeks revenge?'

Mrs Murdstone steadied herself and looked away through the window as the late-evening sun cast its final rays of warmth across her garden.

'I met Ernest the next year. We were married and moved into Laurel House. We had a child. A lovely little girl. We named her May. She was as fresh and bright as the month in which she was born. She was five years old when I saw the grave. It was there in St Peter's in the very same spot. It had May's name on it and the date of her death which was the 8th of June of the same year. It was 1897. I stumbled and fainted. By the time I'd recovered it had gone. I didn't want to believe it. I forced myself to believe I'd had some sort of funny turn because of the stress of losing Alice. I did nothing. I shut it out, and we carried on with our lives.'

'And on the 8th of June she died?'

Edith wiped the tears from her eyes and continued. 'No Adam, she was taken. She was in the garden playing one minute and the next she'd vanished. Then I suddenly heard childish laughter. It was inside my head. It was the laughter of a child who had got her own back: sneering, vindictive. I ran across on to the Moor, and they were there in the distance. May was being led away. I raced as fast as I could to catch them but it seemed like the faster I ran the further away they went. Then they disappeared into the mist. I kept on running, shouting and crying her name but the mist closed in and I was lost. I sat on the grass and cried.'

'Dear, God. What happened next?'

'People must have heard my cries. They came running. Twenty or thirty of them. They swept across the Moor, searching, calling, but there was no trace. The mist lifted and the search went on for hours until it was dark. It carried on the next day and the day after but she was gone. I knew it was Alice but I couldn't say anything, not even to Ernest. She'd cast me into the worst nightmare you could imagine. I deserved it. She should have taken me. She had no need to take May.'

'The picture in my room. You drew it to remind you.'

'It is my two girls, Adam. It was the last time I saw them. It reminds me of the life we could have had.'

'What about Ernest? Where is he now?'

'Ernest died, Adam. He was heartbroken. He searched the Moor day after day, visited neighbouring towns. He was certain she'd been taken by travellers. They were so very helpful. They tried to find her. Sent messages out to all their folk across the country. I had to sit back and watch it all. I just stood and watched his heart break. One night he didn't come home. They found him in the river. The police and the church were kind. They said it was an accident. He's buried in his family plot in Stanport.'

'So Sam Blackwood will be next? He will be the victim of her malevolence. And you are saying he must be in some way connected with you or Joseph. So who is this child? Surely you must have some idea?'

'He shares your name, Adam. He is somehow part of your world, not mine.'

* * * * * *

We took flowers and walked along the river to St Martin's. Neither of us spoke along the way. At the churchyard we made our way towards the grave. It had been some time since my last visit, and I hoped the weeds and undergrowth had not reclaimed the plot to an extent where it would appear untended and neglected.

There was a silence, a stillness of air and sound which gripped the churchyard like a breath held in anticipation of a hallowed moment.

I stopped a few yards away and ushered Edith forward. I could see that the grave was still clearly visible, but the peg doll had disappeared, and I cursed the action of some unholy person who had dared to take it as their own. Edith continued, kneeling in prayer by the grave. I turned and walked back to the church, not wishing to intrude on the moment of reconciliation and the emotions it might bring.

After a few minutes, I was joined by Edith. Some colour had returned to her cheeks, but there were fresh lines of concern on her face.

'She is in unconsecrated ground. I thought that would be the case given that she was born out of wedlock and not baptised.'

'Perhaps we could consult the vicar and seek a way of moving her into the church grounds.'

'Then all would have to be known.' She spoke as if the secrets had to be retained, locked away as they had been for over twenty years. She looked at me earnestly and gripped my arm.

'Will you tell? Do you think this has to be revealed?'

'I need time to think. I will return to Elm House this afternoon and collect my thoughts. Whatever happens, though, you know where she lies. Let me see what I can do. A new vicar is arriving. He knows nothing of Cedar Moor or its history. Perhaps he will agree to move her. That will be of some comfort to you.'

She looked at me with some concern. 'It will be of some comfort to me, Adam. But she is not at rest.'

.

.

Chapter 18
Joseph and The Curse

I left Edith at her home and decided to sit for a while on the Moor to think through the events. I needed to disentangle my thoughts that twisted and constricted my mind. I was suddenly the keeper of information that was not welcome, and I was bitter and angry for bringing the discovery upon myself. My choices were clear. Presume to know nothing and maintain the status quo with the risk that future discovery would cast me as an accomplice to the indiscretions of Edith and Joseph that had directly led to the abandonment and death of a young child. Where would this leave me with Clara? Were the facts to become known would our relationship be forever fragmented and our future together cast into jeopardy?

Alternatively, I could confront Joseph in private, but what this might lead to I was unsure. Would he try to buy me off assuming the power of his money could silence all who might bring his standing into disrepute? Or would he break down and confess, with all the associated distress that would be inflicted on his family?

After an hour of thought, I decided that I had to act within a strict code of morals. Joseph, primarily, and Edith, to a slightly lesser degree, had breached the boundaries of acceptable behaviour. I had to take a strong standpoint so that no criticism could be directed at me. Clara would understand. It would be an almighty shock, but she would accept what I was doing to be right and proper. I would ask to see Joseph in private, reveal what I knew, and how I came about the details. I would gauge his reaction and move on from there.

I entered the driveway but almost before I had time to collect my thoughts, I was greeted by Clara, her face strewn with tears. She flung herself into my arms and in a barely coherent voice delivered the news that Joseph was dead.

The girls were clustered around Mary who sat motionless in a wing-backed chair, the remains of a glass of brandy clasped in her hand. Joseph had collapsed at work. Medical attention had been almost immediate, but there was nothing that could be done. He had been brought back to the house, and the funeral director was to arrive presently.

The greater power of God had allowed my decision to be made. I knew that the secrets I held were to be silenced forever. Edith would lead her life free from the shadow of Joseph and the mistakes of the past. Alice might now lie in peace, and I would try to secure an arrangement that she might be buried in the consecrated ground.

That night I knelt at my bed and prayed. I prayed for Joseph's salvation and the hope that God was the all-forgiving entity that the Bible proclaimed. I prayed that Joseph's death had appeased Alice and that she would find solace in his departure from this world. But my small flicker of hope struggled to gain a secure foothold in my thoughts. Her mother still lived. The woman whose unconditional love had been surrendered to allow Joseph to protect his character, his marriage and his standing in society. It was an unforgivable act, and even as the thoughts tumbled in my mind I could feel a restless energy creeping wilfully through the foundations of our lives.

* * * * * *

The day of Joseph's funeral was grey. There was little light. The colours of summer were muted through a veil of drizzle which soaked the mourners as they gathered at St Peter's. The family had walked to the church, a cluster of black that moved slowly past the edge of the Moor, heads bowed below umbrellas that gave scant protection against the worst of the elements. Along the path to be taken by the horse-drawn hearse, people came from their houses waiting silently at their gates to say farewell to a man whose business had given many of them employment and security.

Edith Murdstone was not there. I had visited her earlier in the week and explained that the events of her past life would remain closed and that no word of the happenings would ever cross my lips. Joseph was dead. The ties had been cut, and there was no need to prolong their relationship into death by her attending the funeral.

I watched the coffin approach through different eyes than those of the many villagers who gazed upon it. They shone with respect, admiration and sympathy for a man they believed to be a pillar of their society: a shining example of all that was good. They knew nothing of the evil that had finally been extinguished. As the coffin was lifted from the carriage, I wondered if he lay in peace.

I wondered too about the words being offered up by the vicar. Did the thanks for a life well-lived spiral up through the body of the church and reach out to the heavens and, if so, did an all-knowing God look down with forgiveness or damnation?

I shivered. The same ominous feelings that I encountered at my wedding seemed to seep into my being. The shadows in the church darkened, and above the knave a slight flicker across the stained-glass window made me glance anxiously up, but it was a momentary distraction and instantly lost.

We followed the coffin bearers from the church and out into the drizzle which continued to cling to our clothes like a damp shroud. We trooped slowly across the sodden grass until we reached the grave. We stood in silence as the wind whipped around the trees, rustling the leaves, producing more shadows which swept across the paths and lawns. And then I saw her, in exactly the same place as she had appeared on my wedding day. Alice, shadow black, the merest of features visible from within the hollow of the cloak. She knelt beside the gravestone where only moments earlier there had been empty space.

I backed away from the mourners who were listening to the words of prayer, rising and falling in the rushes of wind. I moved stealthily around some headstones, moving closer to her without breaking my gaze. Suddenly a wild breeze gathered leaves, twigs and dust from the hollows of the path and swept them across my field of vision. Rain and dust assaulted my eyes, and I was momentarily blinded. By the time I had wiped them clean, she was gone. But the grave remained.

SAM
BLACKWOOD
A beloved child
born............. died 8th June 1902

But then as I looked at the stone it began to change. The moss and lichen began to turn darker and pieces began to wither and fall, losing their grasp and tumbling from the gravestone to the earth. Then came the laughter, barely audible, but unmistakably that of a young child trying to suppress its glee. A child not wishing to reveal its delight in my horror as I read the full inscription trying to believe that my eyes had made some cruel mistake.

LUCY
JESSAMINE
BLACKWOOD
A beloved child
born 14th March 1902 died 8th June 1902

A cold fear gripped me with such intensity that I began to shake. This was no sorrowful soul but a spirit whose thirst for revenge had festered and grown as her earthly flesh lay rotting in an abandoned grave.

There was no Sam Blackwood, no male child born to this earth and destined to die on the date which repeated through the mysteries that had plagued my life for over a year. My interpretation of the inscription was wrong. The name Sam was concealed within the body of Lucy's second name. Andrew's warning on our first meeting had come to pass. Clara and I had become victims of her desire for revenge. The grave was Lucy's. She was destined to meet her untimely death just one month from today, the same date on which this anguished child and May Wood had left this earth.

'Different names appear on the gravestone.' The words of Edith Murdstone leapt into my head causing a wave of panic to course through my body. 'It depends on whoever is next.'

I left Clara with the mourners and ran back to Elm House bursting through the door with such force that Hannah and her helpers came scurrying from the drawing-room. I grabbed Lucy from the clutches of her nanny, and half staggered up the stairs to the bedroom where I slammed and locked the door holding Lucy for all I was worth.

There I stayed until the knock came. It was Clara accompanied by David. They knocked quietly at first and then louder. Between the knocks I could hear Clara crying, sobbing, calling my name and that of Lucy.

I called to David assuring him that we were both all right and asking him to allow me time together with Clara. I heard some mutterings between them both and then footsteps as he left. I lay Lucy on the bed and gently opened the door. I let Clara into the bedroom and locked the door behind her. She was quite exhausted through sobbing and worry. I let her sit on the bed and gather up Lucy before I steadied myself and told her everything. She listened in disbelief, shaking her head in denial when I gave her the details of Edith Murdstone and her father. She wept openly when I told her about Alice.

'This spirit, Adam. It must be from your imagination. Only you have encountered her. It must be as David said. The worry and anxiety have caused your mind to play tricks; to travel to places which exist only in your imagination. There are no ghosts, Adam. We are safe, here within these walls. We need to get on with our lives. Father is dead. I have no intention of inflicting more pain on my mother. You must see David again. He will prescribe you a strong medicine to settle your mind. I will take Lucy down while you rest awhile.'

'No! Can't you understand? We have to get away. We have to leave this damned area before the 8th of June. We have one month. We cannot be here on that date. You must put your trust in me.'

I grabbed the child from her grasp and ran down the stairs and into Joseph's study. We needed money, and I believed Joseph kept substantial sums in his safe. I was frantic, my ability to reason stripped away leaving only fear and the desire to flee from the danger. I searched for a key, emptying the contents of drawers and cupboards until they lay strewn across the floor. The banging on the door seemed distant, muffled, absent from my immediate reality. In my confusion I knocked an expensive jar from the mantelpiece and the key lay with the shattered remains of the pottery, its worth obliterated in my moment of madness. I thrust the key into the lock and grabbed everything inside the safe. There was money. More than enough to help us flee from Cedar Moor for the time required but there were also documents and a death certificate which bore the name, Ellen Marie Longman.

I ripped the contents from the envelope. The white parchment certificate unveiled a horror that only served to fuel my distress and send my emotions spiralling into a pit of dread and despair.

The date of her departure from this earth cut into me like a fatal wound. Born on March 14th 1894, she died on the 8th of June in Edinburgh that same year. Hattie's despair over the birth of Lucy was explained. All female members of Joseph's bloodline, born after Alice's death, were destined to die on the same date as Alice. The exception, of course, was Rosie's daughter, Victoria, who was now a healthy child of seven years. The significance of Rosie being adopted was now clear. Victoria did not share Joseph's bloodline and was safe. Alice's curse was revealed and, with the exception of Grace and Clara, it was known by all in the Jackson family.

But the panic spread deeper as I realised the significance of Ellen Marie's resting place. Hattie and Howard had fled to escape the curse, but Alice had followed as surely as she had tracked my own soul to the grounds of Greyfriars Kirk.

The pounding on the door brought me to my senses. I could hear the voices of Howard and Richard added to that of David who was trying to reason with me through the heavy, oak door I placed Lucy on the couch and clutched the death certificate in my hand.

Slowly I released the lock and pulled back the door. They stood before me, Howard and Richard to the fore, Rosie and Hattie holding Clara next to David and Grace. The dark mass of funeral clothes was broken only by their white faces which stared at me as if they were looking into depths of some inexplicable horror.

'You knew.' I spoke slowly and deliberately to Howard and Hattie. 'You saw a gravestone. The gravestone of Ellen Marie. You knew all this would come to pass when Lucy was born and you chose to stay silent, hiding in the background waiting for the day to come. Have you already rehearsed your offers of condolence? Are your tears already stored away ready to be shed with the dawning of that day?'

Hattie burst into tears. Grace stared uncomprehendingly, not yet party to the story that Joseph had thought would be buried with him as he was lowered into the earth just two hours before.

Richard stepped forward, attempting to gain control of the situation. 'Yes, Adam, we all knew. We hoped the blight upon the family would abate after the death of Ellen-Marie. We believed that if Alice had taken a life for a life, it would all be done.'

'You let people believe I was teetering the edge of insanity.'

Mary spoke earnestly, 'We had no choice, Adam, our standing in the community. We would have been destroyed. Joseph's reputation...'

'To Hell with Joseph's reputation. He is the source of all this. He cared only for himself, to cover his back, to shamefully turn away from a child on the brink of death. To silence a woman and take her child from her. He needs to rot, rot to his very core in a twisted, dark purgatory.'

Blank faces stared back at me. Mary's face was lined with tears which dripped and settled into her lace handkerchief. Grace was led away by David; an innocent woman whose future would be childless unless I could somehow lay Alice Skerry to rest and assure her the debt had been paid.

'I will solve this! This spirit is evil but she is a child cast into anguish and torment and needs to be freed.' I looked at Hattie, 'For all our sakes, I will bring a resting peace to her. You and Howard still have time.'

I shut the door and sat down in contemplation for some time. The light was fading into an evening glow when Clara returned from her counsel with Grace and David. She sat quietly with her hand in mine, holding Lucy close in her arms. She seemed numb, unemotional, perhaps in a state tortured realisation that my story was true and that we now had to face the unthinkable consequences.

Chapter 19
Salvation

We had one month to save our child but we had no knowledge of how to deal with supernatural affairs. All we comprehended was that there was a child who was not at rest. She was a spirit fuelled with vengeance against the living. Whether this desire to punish our family had expired with Joseph's death I knew not. I could not sit and wait idly gazing on my beautiful daughter, the clock ticking relentlessly away, the hours and minutes disappearing with the fading of each evening light. The slow descent of Lucy's life ebbing away towards the fatal day.

My initial thoughts were to put our trust in the church. After all, we were Christians, followers of the faith, and were innocent in all affairs relating to the past life of Joseph Jackson. It had been two days since the funeral, and I had recovered enough strength to nurture a flicker of belief that I could somehow bring Clara and Lucy through this nightmare where we would emerge stronger and free from the overshadowing peril.

I needed to talk to Edith Murdstone again. She had lived for twenty years or more with the consequences of Joseph's actions. Perhaps it was not my sole responsibility to make peace with Alice. If we could talk and identify a common pathway to seek Alice's forgiveness then some faint flicker of hope might rise from the ashes of Joseph's life.

I took Max and we walked briskly across the Moor As on my previous visit, there was no answer when I knocked on the door of Laurel House, but once again I found the door ajar. Again my calls to Edith to warn her of my entry went unheeded. The air inside the house was thick and, there was a silence as if all sound had been banished and time was standing still. Max kept to my side. There was no whimpering or signs of distress but he pulled slightly on the leash as if to lead me towards the stairs.

The house was dark and silent. All the curtains had been drawn. Entering from the brightness of a summer's day my eyes could not seem to get used to the darkness. I lit a candle and carried it through into the hall. My shadow flickered and roamed across the walls. Max pulled tighter leading me across the hallway in the direction of the stairs.

We climbed slowly, our shadows dancing freely across the upper reaches of the stairwell, beckoning us on like two diabolic fiends intent on luring us towards some vile discovery. The only sounds were my muffled footsteps on the carpet and my irregular gasps of breath as I fought to restrain Max whose pull now was becoming substantial. As we reached the top my grip on Max's leash weakened and he broke free scampering across the landing and settling in front of one of the bedrooms.

The door was locked. I pressed my weight against the frame, but it would not budge. I peered through the keyhole. The curtains were drawn, and I squinted into the darkness pressing my eye as close as I could to the metal lock. I held it there waiting for my sight to become used to the gloom. At first, I could only see the outlines of the curtains which protected the room from the direct sunlight. After some seconds my eye gradually began to pick out shapes in the room. There was a chair, what seemed like a broken vase lying on the floor, and the end of the bedstead. Then suddenly a draft of air parted the curtain and protruding from the end of the bed was a foot; a woman's foot which hung limply down from the mattress.

I rushed into the garden, grabbed a spade from the shed, and raced back to the room. I wielded the spade, striking the handle and lock with all my might. I hit it again and again, sweat pouring from my body but driven on by a force which gave me strength beyond my means. At last, the lock cracked. I threw the spade onto the floor and pushed open the door. I was almost driven to retreat by the odour of death and there on the bed lay Edith Murdstone. There was not a mark upon her. She lay on her back, eyes closed, her arms folded in a burial pose. There in her hand was a doll, a child's peg doll. The doll I had left on Alice's grave almost a year ago.

That she was in my presence again there was no doubt. But this time the sound which crept and whispered through the cracks and crevices of the house was not one of laughter but a slow, mournful sobbing that steadily became fainter until all that was left around me was the empty silence of death.

I drew a handkerchief from my jacket and pressed it against my face. Carefully I released the doll from Edith's grip and folded her hand back across her chest. I drew a sheet across her face, stuffed the doll inside my jacket, and made my way to the police station.

* * * * * *

It had to be over. Those responsible for the misery of Alice's short life and her death were gone. I prayed that the doll symbolised the finality of it all and Alice could complete her journey from a world of shadows into one of light, hope and salvation. But the day was there on the calendar, now less than a month away. An immovable omen which ate away at the time which crept ever nearer with each tick of our grandfather clock.

The next two days were desperate. We went to every church in Stanport but could find no help. 'Pray,' was the constant response. 'Put your faith in God, and he will be your saviour.' The words were honest, well-meaning, but they cast more misery upon us. It seemed we had to wait. The days would be struck from the calendar, each pencil mark plunging us into new depths of despair. We knew of no path that could lead us from the dreaded, yet unknown encounter, that lurked on the horizon like some hungry predator.

Late in the evening, there was a knock on the front door. I hesitated to answer at first not wishing to be drawn into social intercourse when my mind was wracked with worry. It was Clara who chose to see who was there. In a few moments, she returned with David who was accompanied by a smartly dressed man who removed his flat-brimmed hat as he entered our sitting room.

'Adam, Clara, I'd like you to meet Frank Collins. He is the brother of a colleague of mine. I think he may be able to help you.'

'Evening, sir. Evening ma'am.' He spoke with a soft American accent. 'If I may introduce myself. As David has said, my name is Frank Collins, and I am a minister in the Church of the Latter-Day Saints. You may have heard of us. We have a strong membership over here in England. David has explained the source of your worries to me. I understand what you must be going through at this most troublesome time. I am not without experience in such matters. I understand that your little girl is in grave danger. Would you like me to explain how I may help?'

I was wary. My experience of Americans came from tales of travelling shows. The connection with Joseph and his arrangements for Alice were worrying. This man did not

170

look like a minister. He dressed in the smart clothes of a city broker who had the means to indulge in fine tailoring. I was concerned about how he acquired his wealth and if his 'help' involved me in parting with a substantial amount of money, but we listened closely. Frank spoke softly, his voice giving an air of quiet reassurance.

'I understand you feel that the child, Alice Skerry, is not at rest and you are seeking to find a mutual peace. In my mind, the child cannot separate you from Joseph. You are his kin, Clara, you share his blood and lineage. You are a living part of him. The child will feel that, and that is why she will not rest. We need to build a bridge between you both which will result in that separation. A parting of the ways that leads everyone to peace. I believe the child lies in unconsecrated ground and that no baptism was granted to her. This will cause her restlessness. There is no pathway to God. We must provide a direction for her journey which leads her away from her purgatorial existence. There is a way. My church can provide it.'

Clara squeezed my hand. She looked at me, and I could see the desperation in her eyes. She nodded gently and turned towards Frank.

'Mr Collins. We would like to hear you out. We seem to have little option other than to wait for the inevitable.'

Frank leant across and placed his hand on hers. 'My church has a doctrine for the baptism of the dead. We have practised such since 1840. It offers baptism by proxy to those who died without the opportunity to receive it. It is currently practised across our church but only in one of our dedicated temples. Our view is that every person has the right to enter the Kingdom of God.'

'What do you mean by baptism by proxy?'

'It is baptism by immersion, performed by a living person acting on behalf of one who is dead.'

He continued with the details, and we listened in hope. The ceremony would take place at their nearest temple which was in Preston. The person acting as a proxy would have to be a member of the church and the same sex as the deceased. He recommended his daughter, Sarah, of twelve years who he said had participated before. He could arrange the ceremony without delay as soon as we could provide him with as many details as we could about Alice. It would be an advantage if something belonging to her was there at the time to allow a secure connection between this world and the next.

'Will we have any indication that the baptism has worked and that she is at peace?'

He looked at us solemnly. 'There are no guarantees, I'm afraid. Our belief is that those who have died may choose to accept or reject the baptisms done on their behalf.'

'How soon would we know?'

Frank spoke earnestly. 'Forgive me, but I think you have the answer to that question already. The 8th of June, no later than midnight. That is when you will know.'

* * * * * *

After the meeting with Frank, I sought out Andrew. We had not met since the mystery of Alice and Sam Blackwood had been resolved. There was now no puzzle that needed to stretch his academic wisdom, but I felt the need to explore his opinions on Frank's church. I wondered how he might view its beliefs, its theory of surrogate baptism and the subsequent impact on Alice's restless spirit. We met in his study at the university and he listened intently, his eyes flickering with interest as each stage of the mystery was revealed.

His voice was one of concern and his brow furrowed.

'You will need to tread carefully, Adam. The Church in question is a controversial undertaking by Americans who, shall we say, have no tangible foundation on which to spread their doctrine. Its source was the supposed discovery of a golden book. It was rumoured to contain the religious beliefs of an ancient people and subsequently translated and published as the *Book of Mormon*. I would think carefully about any temptation to become involved with them. They are an unknown force both in this world and the next.'

'Can I ask your honest opinion of the baptism by proxy. It seems to be our only hope.'

'I have heard of it. It is an interesting belief which, if successful, can I believe bring some comfort to both parties. But it is undoubtedly a risk, Adam. What it stirs in the purgatorial cauldron of the unknown may contain grave elements of danger.'

'What are my options?'

'I have no answers, Adam. You must either go through with the baptism or do nothing. Either way, the 8th of June will decide your fate, but I must warn you of one thing.'

'What is that?'

'If the 8th of June passes without harm coming to you or your family, it will mean that Alice's spirit is at rest. Either the deaths of Joseph Jackson and Edith Murdstone will have already secured her peace, or the baptism has offered her similar comfort. If the date passes without incident, she is at rest. It is over. You will be able to move once more in peaceful ways. But heed this carefully.'

He moved swiftly to the shelves stacked behind his desk and without hesitating lifted a small volume from a row of battered, brown books. I caught the title as he placed it squarely on the table, *The Science of the Spirit World*, by his mentor, A R Campbell Brown.

'Listen carefully. It is imperative that you take this advice.' He moved his glasses to the bridge of his nose and read,

'Spirits who furtively search for rest are directionless and unpredictable. They may, on the one hand, be merely mischievous but on the other angry and malevolent souls determined to strike and harm those who they consider responsible for their plight. Should they be laid to rest, they must be left in peace. Their graves should be left unattended and abandoned by all who the spirit perceives were connected with the source of their discomfort.'

He closed the book and looked into my eyes. 'I will pray, Adam, that you sleep well on the night of the 8th of June and awake to a new beginning. Remember, if that happy day should dawn neither you, or any members of your family, should return to Alice's grave. She will be at rest, and you must leave her as such.'

He shook my hand, placed his arm around my shoulder and guided me from his study out into the light of a glorious summer's afternoon.

'Take care on your journey.'

'I will. When all this is over you must come and visit us at Glamis House.'

I suddenly felt his grip weaken in my hand.

'Your house is named Glamis?'

'Indeed. It was named by the previous owner. A business associate of Joseph's from Scotland. Do you know of the name?'

'By God I do, Adam, it is one of Scotland's most famous castles. It is said to be one of the most haunted places in the land.'

I quickly told him about the Bryants and young Jack's belief that he was the victim of a sinister trick played by his sister.

There was deep concern in Andrew's eyes. 'The Scotsman. He must have seen her. She may have been visiting the house for some time. In the legend of Glamis, there are several reports of children waking in the middle of the night to find a dark figure standing over their beds. But why would she be there before your arrival, Adam?'

I could offer no logical response to Andrews's question and I left for home. The light was mellowing as I strolled from the station. The Moor seemed at peace and the air was still. I wanted to capture this moment and weave it into a world where I could settle with my family, untroubled by the events that now seemed to blight our future. I reached the end of Park Grove and stopped in front of the gates looking at our home which sat splendidly amongst the lofty trees and mature plants in their full bloom of summer.

I gazed at the name. Glamis. It was carved into a thick piece of oak and had been nailed to another piece which in turn was attached to the gatepost. The piece behind was old and the exposed wood was surrendering to the elements with strands of white fungus stretching along the weathered edges. At one end the nails attaching the new nameplate were beginning to rust and their hold had begun to loosen providing sufficient space for me to insert my fingers and create enough purchase to prize the sign away from its elder companion.

I stepped back, holding the newer sign, unaware that my grip was loosening and it was sliding from my grasp. The old sign remained attached to the gatepost, the wood was beginning to crack and split but its painted, gold lettering was still visible. Shaw House. It was the previous address of Edith Wood. The one I saw on a letter on her bureau when I first came to Cedar Moor. We were living in the very house occupied by Edith at the time of Alice's death. Her presence was explained. She would know every inch of our home. If the baptism failed, she would be with us on the 8th of June. Of that, there could be little doubt.

.

Chapter 20
Despair

The train laboured out of Victoria Station, squealing and rattling across the matrix of rails which directed it away from the main lines and onto a suburban journey through the northern outskirts of the city. The faithful Max lay at my feet. I stroked his head gently. He seemed calm and at ease, in stark contrast to the feelings of uncertainty which were knotting inside me. We conversed little on the journey, preferring to immerse ourselves in our thoughts as we passed row upon row of terraced houses until eventually swathes of greenery finally asserted themselves, and we picked up speed under the shadow of Winter Hill. Bulbous black clouds rolled across its summit. The sky seemed low as if it wished to descend and smother our intentions but the train sped on and with it our hopes too gathered momentum. The sky brightened, and in less than an hour the train heaved to a halt and the guard announced our arrival at Preston Station.

The town was busy, and we hailed a cab to take us on the short journey to the temple. Anxiously, I checked my bag, to make sure the peg doll was still inside. It was the sole possession that would connect Alice with her proxy. Without it, we had no hope of accomplishment and deliverance.

Presently we drew up in a street of red brick houses and alighted from the cab. On the opposite side of the road was what appeared to be an old schoolhouse. It seemed to have undergone some modification. The gate to the outer yard was freshly painted and the stonework clean and restored. In the centre of the building the bell tower had been raised and atop it sat a short spire pointing at the heavens from which droplets of rain began to gently fall. Frank greeted us at the gate.

'The dog will need to remain outside; we cannot risk any disruption to the ceremony.'

I patted Max gently and wrapped his lead around a nearby wooden post. 'Stay, Max, stay.' I stroked him softly to provide some reassurance and he responded by licking my hand. There was a slight quivering in his body. Whether this was fear or cold I could not be certain but he settled to the ground to await my return.

'Come this way.' Frank ushered us through the gates and through the heavy oak doors which parted with surprising ease. Inside the building had been converted into the layout of a church except that the seats were modern and arranged in four rows which ran the length of the building on either side of the aisle.

At the front of the church stood two men, a woman and a young girl. She was wearing a white dress with long sleeves, and her hair was tied back neatly with a white bow. She stood behind the woman who Frank introduced as Ruth, his wife.

'And this is Sarah, our daughter. She has kindly offered to be baptised in proxy of Alice. This here is Mr William Stringer who is our minister who will conduct the baptism and this is Mr Jesse Swift who will assist with the service. Would you like to proceed, gentlemen?'

William Stringer took hold of Sarah's hand. We were instructed to sit at the head of the aisle, watching, praying, and clinging to the hope that a spirit that had drifted into to darkness could be finally released from the shadows of its restless existence.

At the end of the aisle stood a large stone font. Frank explained that the church believed that every part of the body needed to be immersed in the water to establish a full and unbroken bond of faith with resurrection and eternal life. I watched as Sarah moved slowly down the aisle, her eyes focused on the minister who waited by the font, the peg doll clutched tightly in her left hand.

She reached the font. The minister guided her onto a stone step, and she made the first contact with the water as her foot moved tentatively into the font. She was shivering, or perhaps shaking with fear. Both legs were inside the rim now, and as the minister spoke, she descended until only her head was above the waterline with her black hair floating around her.

'Give me your hand child.'

She raised her right arm from the font, the water cascading down the white material, tight and transparent against her skin. He took the peg doll and folded her fingers around it.

Immediately, he placed his hand directly on the top of Sarah's head and plunged her down into the water. She sank into the font disappearing in a swirl of white. A wash of water burst against the sides of the marble sending waves breaking and spilling across the aisle, and I could see her distorted shape floundering under the force of minister's grasp.

'In the name of Alice Skerry, I baptise you in the name of the Father, and of the Son, and of the Holy Spirit.'

She was lifted gasping and crying from the water. Ruth moved quickly from the edges of the aisle and wrapped her trembling body in towels.

There was a moment of cold silence and then came the rumbling. From directly above there was a sound, as something slithered above our heads, gathering volume and momentum as it descended swiftly across the rafters, echoing in the roof space. I grasped Clara's hand, and we both looked towards the light filtering through the grey slates

179

directly above. The rumbling got louder, the movement swifter, until suddenly there was silence which was broken moments later by a splintering crash, the sound of fragments ricocheting off the church door, and a cry that rose and ceased in almost an instant.

I leapt from my seat, rushed to the door and flung it open. By my feet lay the body of a large, grey squirrel its head removed by the slate which had hurtled from the roof like a guillotine blade. It lay like some pagan sacrifice at my feet still quivering, blood spouting from the arteries that only moments ago had infused its body with life. There was no sign of Max. His lead had been severed by the slate which must surely have been meant for him. Then more rumblings came and another slate hurtled earthwards embedding itself in the soft soil just inches from where I stood. I heard a whimpering in the hedgerow and saw Max cowering in fear I grabbed what remained of his lead and hurled him with some force towards me and into my arms. Then I ran as the noise from above grew louder and more slates flew from the roof like blades hurled by the Devil himself.

I slammed the door shut barring the way to the others who had followed me in concern. I motioned to Clara, and we ran, down the aisle and out of the door at the rear of the building. We ran until we reached the station, tears coursing down our faces until we climbed into a carriage trembling and shaking with a panic which only abated as the train pulled safely away from the platform.

* * * * * *

I prayed that the attempt to inflict harm on Max and myself was a final, spiteful gesture from a petulant child. A symbol of her angry suffering and torment directed at us because of our connection to those responsible for her death. I could only pray that the door had now been slammed shut and that the passageway between this world and the next was locked and bolted forever. But the silence between us confirmed that we feared the worst; that Alice was not now the innocent child who had needlessly died because of Joseph's callous act. As the years passed, her spirit had grown restless and unforgiving, her desire to inflict revenge fed by a bitter hatred of those who had abandoned her.

I gazed from the train at a storm sweeping in above Winter Hill. The clouds gathered, constricting the light as our silent journey continued. As the minutes ebbed away, even the shadows that symbolised my fear would soon become swallowed up in the darkness.

Chapter 21
June 8th 1902

There was no light now. The hope and anticipation of the baptism had faded, and we were left in darkness; a world of torment where we had no means of knowing which path our lives would take after the despised date that would arrive in twelve hours time.

Frank had arrived back from Preston with the baptism certificate for Alice and a conviction that we must still cling to hope and that incident with the slates was but a mere coincidence: an inevitable consequence of the danger surrounding an old building which was in need of some repair.

I could take no comfort from his optimism. There had been no signs that Alice was at rest, or indeed had any desire to cease her vengeful quest. We would have to see the day through in an environment where all normal risks of death were removed. We would spend the hours locked in the main bedroom of our house. I had gathered a supply of food and water. Amongst other things, I had towels, bandages, cigarettes, matches, whisky, a Bible and a gun.

At 10pm I took Clara and Lucy upstairs. We fed her warm milk and settled her into her cot. The time ticked away. With five minutes of the day left, we were ready. Max settled at my feet. The hands on the clock moved towards midnight. We fixed our eyes upon it, held our breath and prayed.

The first chimes of the grandfather clock filled the hall with echoes. Twelve strikes and then silence. I waited, expecting what, I knew not. Perhaps some instant, catastrophic shaking of the house, a suffocating appearance of spirits from the other side or just the slow expiration of Lucy's life as she slept in the cot. There was nothing. I sat awake through the dark hours listening to the breathing of Clara and Lucy, which was magnified in the silence but filled the room with a comforting confirmation of life.

The gun sat next to me on the bed. I clutched the Bible in my hands, occasionally reading verses to calm me and connect me with faith and the hope that somehow Alice was at rest, our presence at Glamis House, and the deeds of Joseph, now an irrelevance to her spirit.

The early morning passed peacefully. The dawn was clear and bright and promised one of those hot June days where stillness hangs in the air as the heat rises, creating a haze from the dispersion of the morning dew. Lucy woke at around 7am, and Clara changed and dressed her after which she settled her on the rug where she entertained her with playthings and the bonding chatter that passes between mother and daughter.

Clara and I spoke little. We were on edge, alert to every sound and movements of light and shade that passed across the room as the day progressed. Still, there was nothing. We waited as the midpoint of the day arrived and passed silently into the afternoon.

We stayed close to Lucy, watching the doors and windows, peering into the garden, across to the Moor and up into the clouds. Outside it was a weekend like any other. Neighbours chatted on the street corner and children galloped excitedly into the park, free from their parents' reins. The day drifted on, easing into the tranquillity of a late Sunday afternoon.

Just after 4pm, the clouds began to mass across the Pennines which were visible from our elevated position in the house. The light mellowed as the storm brewed. Darkness began to settle on Cedar Moor, and the damp-smelling air became still, almost overbearing, as an ominous silence hung across the gardens, trees and hedgerows. The mournful cry of some woodland creature carried across the Moor and the clouds spat out their first beads of rain which bounced across the roofs sending early rivulets of water scurrying into the drains and gutters.

I had no doubt that she had come. Max began to whine. His ears flattened and the hair on the back of his neck bristled. The room felt oppressive as if an overbearing presence was with us. I felt hot and tired, helpless to do anything other than sit rigidly in the centre of the room. My hand weakened, and the gun fell to the floor. The pages of the Bible rippled as a draught swept down the chimney sending streaks of soot and wisps of dust across the hearth.

The sound of distant thunder rumbled across the rooftops, and the room was suddenly lit by a burst of jagged lightning which brought the rain; torrents of water that sent people running at speed to the shelter of nearby doorways.

I tried to shut it out, drawing the curtains and wedging the fireguard across the chimney. The room was getting hotter, and I wiped the sweat from my brow desperately trying to clear my mind and think as clearly as I could.

Suddenly Clara's cry brought me back to my senses.

'Adam! Adam! For God's sake look!'

I turned and gazed at Lucy who, despite the cauldron of noise and flashes of light was still sleeping in her cot. She looked at peace, content, breathing slowly. Next to her was the peg doll which I had last seen cold and sodden, clutched in Sarah's hand after the baptism.

'Adam! Adam! What shall we do?'

'Wait here!'

I seized the doll and ran from the room with Max at my heels. I grabbed my coat and we ran out into the rain, drenched to the core within seconds of leaving the house.

But still, we ran, the child's doll dripping in my hand as we left the street for the path to the Mersey. I stumbled and slid twice before I reached the river, my clothes filthy with the mud and grass stains. The driving rain thrashed against the surface of the water as the wind rose ripping leaves and twigs from the trees that were hurled into our path, stinging my face and obscuring my vision.

We arrived at St Martin's Churchyard struggling to gain any balance on the paths which were now rivers of rain testing my every move. We drove on through the gate. Now there was no hesitancy from Max, no fear of entering the area of unconsecrated ground. I sank to my knees in front of Alice's grave, washed clean by the storm which was rising in intensity. I took the doll and laid it by the headstone. Then inexplicably I started digging the surface of the grave with my bare hands. Max jumped by my side, clawing at the earth with his paws and panting hard. I pulled away a foot of soil, grabbed the doll and thrust it into the earth. I scooped up the sods and pushed them back into place, burying the doll, and finally hammering with my fists to make sure it was entombed just beneath the surface. Then I pulled the baptism certificate from my coat. It was sodden, and the ink was already bleeding into the parchment, but I stared at the grave and read, 'On this day the 21st of May 1902 Alice Skerry was baptised into the kingdom of God where she will be forever in his family.' Lightning flashed and crackled above me. The church tower was hit sending a cascade of cobalt-blue sparks showering across the churchyard. Shadows appeared and disappeared darting like dervishes between the graves, throwing me into confusion as my eyes followed them across the churchyard. I scrambled to my feet and we fled, spattering mud in all directions as we half ran through the swirls of water that swept in torrents across our path.

The river was unrecognisable now. The force of the rain had turned the surface into a heaving, boiling mass of bubbles and foam. Creatures scurried across the path, desperate for shelter in the woods and undergrowth. A dead bird thudded to the ground before me, its feathers torn and shredded with the force of the deluge.

I threw myself through the door of Glamis House, pulling Max with me, and collapsing in the hall, a pool of water forming from my sodden garments. Clara rushed from the bedroom and slammed and bolted the front door. She wrapped Max in a towel and helped me up to the bedroom where I sat gasping and exhausted before yielding to sleep and sinking into its dark depths.

I awoke in a panic. I dared not open my eyes but when I summoned the courage the room was filled with light, the rays of a thin morning sun creeping through the gaps in the curtains. The gun and the Bible lay next to me on the bed. The room was deathly still, the silence broken only by the steady breathing that drifted from the armchair in the corner. There sat Clara holding Lucy. They were both in the clutches of sleep lying contentedly, swathed in a warm blanket. The faithful Max lay at my feet. The clock on the wall was silent. There was no ticking to break into the calm of a new morning. The hands had stopped some hours earlier at one minute after midnight.

I drew the curtains looking out at the mist that lay across the reaches of the Moor. The sun was fighting to gain a foothold in the day which promised to be clear and warm. I moved to the wall where the calendar hung. It had been a burden on our lives for the past thirty-one days, each one with the exception of the 8th of June crossed out reluctantly in the countdown to what we perceived the inevitable death of our child. I took a pen from the desk and struck through the date. It would not be the date of Lucy's death. The date of the premonition on the gravestone was gone. The time had passed.

.

Chapter 22
The Girl on the Moor

Two years went by and our life was joyous. Lucy was now a beautiful child and had developed her own character and a love of life. Our second child, Henry, was now nine months old and our family was complete. I had risen to the top of my profession. Mr Tomkins had retired, and I was now the respected manager of the local bank. We had settled into our delightful home, restoring its name to Shaw House, and were very much members of a thriving and prosperous community. Alice had been reinterred within the grounds of St Martin's. I could not return to see the plot but was assured by the Reverend Powell that it was kept clean and tidy by the sexton. I felt at peace with everything, in this world and the next.

Grace and David's daughter, Emma, had arrived in the world just one month earlier. The family was delighted even though the presence of girls in the family did not sit easily with Thomas, who saw them as troublesome creatures who might interrupt his manly games of football or hoop and stick.

On this day all the family were together and Elm House was alive with the chatter and noise that children seem to generate when surrounded by each other. We assembled in the drawing-room and Mary had arranged drinks and a small toast to the memory of Joseph on another special day for us all; the christening of Emma.

I stepped back, detaching myself from the chat that drifted into the background as my thoughts returned to the day in Preston over two years ago when Clara and I seemed to be on a precipice of despair. How our lives had changed since then. We were part of a close-knit family who had pulled together after the death of Joseph and the revelations of the past. We were particularly supportive of Hattie, who I often caught gazing at Lucy. I knew what must be in her thoughts. Could her daughter have been saved? It was a subject I could not bring myself to broach with her, so things remained unsaid. Time was moving on quickly, and I hoped they would be able to come to terms with their grief if such a thing were possible.

Thomas had been granted the day to take Max and explore with his friends, so we left the younger children with Hannah and took the short walk from Elm House to St Peter's Church. David and Grace carried Emma with them. She was dressed in christening clothes and wrapped in a white, knitted shawl lovingly made by Mary. The day was bright, if a little breezy, but everything was in full bloom, and the summer light crept through the trees and the shadows danced around us.

No one had spoken about Alice Skerry and the relationship between Joseph and Edith. All was consigned to history now. Laurel House had been sold and was now owned by a prosperous family who had moved from the northern suburbs of Manchester. Mary seemed to have come to terms with the past and had taken on a new purpose in life, managing Elm House and devoting herself to her grandchildren. The old days were not re-visited. There was nothing there for any of us. We looked to the future and long and prosperous lives.

It was gratifying to see so many friends and local people at the church. It was that sort of community: one which liked to share in the joy and celebrations of others. For the next few days, Grace and David would be the talk of the village before their attention was drawn to other matters of a religious or communal nature.

It was good to see Andrew here too. He had become very much part of my life since moving from Edinburgh to complete his studies at Manchester University. I felt it strange how we had met through that chance encounter in Edinburgh Library. Our purposes in life at that time had been drawn together by the whims of fate. He had shared my journey. Now we had reached the end, but our friendship would last a lifetime.

The church was hushed as the words of the baptism ceremony were delivered. The building seemed bright and alive, the sun streaming through the stained glass window, throwing a kaleidoscope of colours across the nave and along the aisle. Emma was lifted towards the font, cradled in the arms of the vicar, the drops of holy water smoothed across her forehead securing the faith that would protect and guide her in the life to come.

I chose to ignore the slight shadow that drifted across the window and the restlessness of David as he seemed distracted and unfocused on the events. I chose to ignore the signs from Andrew as he tried to gain my attention from a few rows back along the aisle. And I chose to ignore the wind that had suddenly increased in strength whipping and whistling through the high rafters of the church and extinguishing the candle that only moments before had been lit by David and Grace.

The members of the congregation strolled out into the bright sunlight. For a moment time seemed to slow, and I stood as if I was a distant watcher of an event of which I felt no part.

I was brought back to the present by Andrew who grasped my arm and led me away from the crowd.

'Did you feel it in there, Adam?' His hand was shaking and his voice wavering with concern.

He looked me in the eye. 'For pity's sake, man, you didn't go back. You didn't make a new connection after the 8th of June?'

I was about to confirm that I had never returned but my arm was grabbed by Thomas, a mischievous grin lighting up his face.

'Uncle Adam, look what we found in Dunsbury.'

He held in his hand a peg doll. The wood had faded and cracked and its clothes were stained and shredded but there were the long strands of dark hair and the cap with a pink ribbon. The white dress with the embroidered rose was still recognisable, retaining the appearance of a young angel.

'We found it just outside St Martin's Churchyard, Uncle Adam. Someone must have lost it a long time ago.'

He gazed at the look of disbelief in my eyes, bowed his head and took a step backwards. 'I should have left it there, shouldn't I, Uncle Adam?'

The warmth of the day suddenly seemed to fade and a distant rumbling directed my gaze across the Moor where the darkness of a storm was gathering pace.

I snatched the doll from him with unreasonable force, immediately regretting my actions. 'I'm sorry. Look at the clouds. A storm is coming. Get inside where you will be safe.'

Thomas took Max and fled as thunder swept across the skies and the first drops of rain fell with intent. The congregation moved swiftly back into the cover of the church as the clouds cast shadows across the Moor, obscuring the margin between earth and sky, draining the graveyard of its earthly sounds and shapes.

I tried desperately to gather my thoughts and prayed that she had not come for Lucy. Was I certain she was here? Was the curse resurrected, or was the atmosphere in the church all part of a subconscious invention of a mind still suffering the scars of a tortured journey? But Andrew had felt it too, and in an instant, my questions were answered.

In the dim, grey light, she was there, standing motionless as the storm gathered. I looked at Andrew. His eyes were fixed, on the spot where Alice stood, gazing in disbelief as her presence shifted and blurred with every gust of wind and blinding sheet of rain.

Cautiously I moved towards her. This time there seemed to be no gravestone, no resting place for a child destined to die on the 8th June. She remained unmoved as I approached until we were just yards apart. She looked into my eyes and for the first time, I felt no malice or weakening of my spirit.

'Alice.' I held out the doll. I craved some response. Some emotion that might be reflected in her eyes. Something to announce that all was forgiven or that she was at peace, but there was nothing. I felt an overpowering need to make contact with her but suddenly a pair of strong hands restrained my movements. I felt Andrew's grip on my sodden clothes as I was wrestled away and dragged back in the direction of the church.

'Come away, Adam. This is madness. You have no understanding of what demons you could release by bridging the gap between our mortal world and hers.'

'Alice!' I shouted above the thunder which now rolled above us. My voice carried in the wind but her gaze dropped from mine. She turned and slowly moved away towards the Moor, each step diminishing her shape and form.

There was no sense in attempting to pursue her. No way in which I might seek an understanding of the purpose of her reappearance. I would be left to suffer the consequences of her reawakening, however unthinkable they might be. The doll hung limply in my hand, beads of water shaking from my fingers as I trembled with cold and confusion.

I turned to speak to Andrew but suddenly there was a flash of black and white which rushed by my side, ripping the doll from my grasp, and driving on into the storm. It was Max travelling at some speed in the footsteps of Alice.

'No, Max! Stop!'

In seconds he was no more than a distant blur as he closed on Alice, their shapes converging on the dark edges of the Moor, shadow chasing shadow; until the wind drove in a curtain of mist which closed around them, and they were gone.

The rain stopped and the Moor lay silent, dark and empty. I looked at Andrew. His face was white, his eyes fixed on the point where they had disappeared.

'Let them go. This is beyond our understanding.'

Through the deluge, I could see the lights of the church and some distorted figures looking out from the canopy of the chapel. I moved ahead of Andrew resigned to fabricating some half-believable tale as to why the two of us were content to surrender to the elements when reason would dictate that we should have sought shelter.

Cold and exhausted we were gathered into the church. Blankets and hot tea were fetched and we were taken to the vestry to recover. Clara stared at me in disbelief. I was the same wet and bedraggled soul who had stumbled exhaustedly through the door of Glamis on that June night two years ago. But this time there was no Max by my side. He had crossed the boundary between this world and whatever lay beyond.

I looked up at Clara whose face was lined with worry. She looked back not wanting to hear of the events that she knew

I had witnessed. I held her hand tightly. 'Max ran off into the storm. I fear that he is gone.'

She sat beside me, wrapping a dry blanket around my shoulders in the hope it would arrest my shaking and we sat in silence until Thomas wandered casually through the door and stood before us.

'Uncle Adam. Shall I take Max home now the storm has ended? He is waiting for me outside.'

I rose swiftly from my chair and hurried from the church. There was Max, lying in a patch of sunlight. I whistled, and he jumped up and trotted obediently towards me. I sank to my knees cradling his head in my arms. His coat was matted, his fur slippery and wet, but his eyes were bright and alive. Tied to his collar was a piece of pink ribbon.

.

Lightning Source UK Ltd.
Milton Keynes UK
UKHW020656050820
367736UK00010B/346

9 781787 233652